MARIE-HÉLÈNE LeBEAULT

AUTHOR OF THE BLOOD MAGICK TRILOGY

GHOST STORIES

STORIES TO KEEP YOU UP AT NIGHT

BEACHES AND TRAILS
PUBLISHING

GHOSTED

1

SILAS DIDN'T NEED his parents to say it. He had seen that look on his father's face too many times. At fourteen, his parents had made it so often that it was all he had ever known. They had been in their current home for almost five years. It was the first time Silas had had friends. Jake, Louise, Caroline, and Ben. Silas pushed his peas across his plate mindlessly, tapping his foot against the chair leg as he waited for the news he knew was coming.

"Silas, there is something your dad and I want to talk to you about," his mother began.

"We are moving again, aren't we?" Silas asked, keeping his eyes on his peas, suddenly no longer hungry.

"We are, yes," his mother replied.

"Why?" Silas asked, getting annoyed.

"I lost my job a few months ago, and while your mother brings in enough to pay the bills, it's still not enough. I've searched and searched, and there are no jobs in my industry here, so we are moving to a small town down south called Golden-Vale. It has everything a young boy could want. Lots of woodlands to explore and build forts with your friends...." his father tried to explain, but Silas didn't want to hear it.

"I have friends here! You promised we wouldn't have to move again. I don't want to move!" Silas snapped, slamming his fist on the table, struggling to keep the tears in his eyes from falling.

"You will make new friends," his father said.

"I don't want to make new friends. I like my friends. These are the first real friends I've had," Silas croaked.

"I'm sorry, son, but you adjusted once. You can adjust again," his mother smiled sympathetically.

Silas always felt better when talking with his mother. He knew she hated moving as much as he did. But for the love of his father, Silas' mother always put on a smile and did everything she could to support her husband's tech dreams.

"When do we move?" Silas asked, pushing his peas around his plate again.

Both his parents fell quiet, staring at each other as if telepathically arguing over who was to break the bad news.

"Mom? Dad?" Silas asked, worried that no one had answered him.

"Next week," his mother finally answered.

Silas jumped to his feet and ran to his room, slamming the door hard behind him and shutting out his mother's concerned voice as she yelled after him. Then, turning the key, Silas locked the door. He knew his mother too well. She would follow him upstairs and try to comfort him. But now that his door had a lock, he could happily be left alone. Jumping onto his bed, Silas wrapped his pillow around his face. He sobbed into his pillow to drown out his cries. He ignored his mother's persistent knocking and pleas for him to open the door.

"WHAT? Next week? But that's the start of spring break. What about our plans? What about the Cloudy Breeze concert?" Jake complained when Silas broke the news.

"Jake! Don't be so selfish. How are you feeling, Silas?" Caroline asked, rubbing a hand across Silas' back.

"How do you think I feel? I don't want to move; I don't want to leave you guys," Silas groaned, kicking an empty soda can across the yard, ignoring the annoyed glare of the teacher on yard duty.

"We're not kids anymore. We can meet up on weekends. Golden-Vale can't be that far, right? We can jump the bus," Louise chirped enthusiastically.

Silas smiled at the idea that between social media, video chat, and seeing his friends on the weekends. Perhaps this move wouldn't be as bad as the others.

"Wow, Golden-Vale is thirteen hours away by train. It will probably be even more by bus," gasped Ben as he searched for the small town online.

Silas and his friends all grew quiet. This was the end of their group, their gang, and all the plans they had for the future. All the things they had planned for spring break were gone with only a few words. The group complemented each other so well. While one group member was loud, another was soft and quiet. One was intelligent and analytical, while another was a dreamer. They picked each other up when they were down, helped each other learn and grow, and never worried about being anyone but themselves. They were a little family, and it broke their hearts that the family would be no more.

"You aren't moving for a week, right? How about we come and help you pack, and then we all have a weekend sleepover at my house and try to do as many fun things we planned for spring break as we can?" Louise smiled.

"That sounds awesome! And you know what, with social media, we will never be far apart. We can still talk every day. You are not escaping the gang that easily, Silas," Caroline smiled as she hugged Silas tightly.

Ben and Jake had teased that Silas and Caroline would marry one day. They were the group's unofficial couple – Never actually dating, but the pair had been close. Now neither would ever find out if love would blossom.

Over the following days, as the friends pooled together to help Silas pack up his room, they reminisced over old pictures of birthday parties, trinkets won from the arcade, and school trophies. The atmosphere soured as the memories came flooding back and things would never be the same again. Spring break usually marked a few weeks of freedom and fun; now, it marked the breakup of true friendship.

2

SILAS' parents tried to get him to talk on the journey to their new home. But no matter how hard they tried, Silas kept his mouth shut and ignored them, spending most of the journey hiding his tears. He watched his old life fade into the past. The big city slipped to the suburbs, the suburbs gave way to country roads, and Silas was in a completely different world before he knew it. Scrolling through social media, he wiped away his tears before sleep took hold, and he slept the rest of the journey to Golden-Vale.

"Silas, wake up. We are here," his mother urged, gently nudging his knee to wake him up.

Rubbing his eyes, Silas looked out the car window as his father drove up a long, lonely path surrounded by trees. The road was bumpy and uneven, causing the slowly roaming car to shake like an old horse-drawn carriage. Finally, his father stopped the car to get out and open the two rickety rusted gates that protected their property.

Who are we protecting ourselves from? We live miles away from anywhere, Silas thought, rolling his eyes at his mother's overzealous enthusiasm.

"When we get a chance, those gates will need replacing," his father said, grabbing a tissue from the glove box to clean off his hands.

After the gates, the drive up to the house was about five minutes. The house sat in the middle of acres of woods. Silas shimmied across the car's back seat to look out the other window. He struggled to see through the trees but caught a small glimpse of a stream running through their property. As they pulled to the house, Silas spotted an old car that looked frozen in time, half buried by nature. The tree branches had long since destroyed the windows. The old fabric roof was torn, and the interior was covered in leaves and insects.

"That's going to be a job getting rid of. Looks like it will have to be dug out of the earth," his mother said, pointing to the car and scrunching her nose in disgust.

"No, don't. Let's clean it up; it will be cool," Silas insisted.

His imagination ran wild. He could picture himself in the front seat pretending to drive. He knew Caroline and Louise would love it when they visited, and Ben and Jake would think it was super cool. Running over, he snapped pictures, instantly sending them to his friends.

"Okay, Silas, you win. The old creepy car stays," his mother laughed as she began to unpack the car.

DURING THE FIRST few days in their new home, his parents packed and settled in. Still determined not to leave his group of friends behind, Silas left most of his room packed as he explored the new house, documenting every unusual and creepy thing he could to report back to his friends.

The house was rich with history – A wooden, gothic style three-story house with a porch at the back and a wrap-around porch covering from the front door around the left side. It needed a minor repair but nothing his father couldn't handle. Silas entered the kitchen from the back porch after a struggle with the broken door. The kitchen cabinets were falling off their hinges, and the floor needed replacing. Silas rolled his eyes as he snapped pictures.

"Of all the houses they could have bought, why choose this one?" Silas sent in a voice note sending a picture of the kitchen.

"It has character," Louise replied.

"Think of the history, dude; it's kinda cool," Ben enthused.

"No, I agree, it's creepy," Caroline said.

"Show us more," Jake insisted, his excitement evident.

Silas explored the house further. A door at the back of the kitchen led onto a large open dining room with five tall windows letting in an abundance of light.

Well, this is kinda cool, I guess, Silas thought, snapping a selfie to send his friends.

"Dude, you should document your house on Instagram. These creepy pictures will definitely grow your followers," Jake sent in a voice note.

"Good idea. Thanks, dude," Silas smiled, uploading his first few pictures.

The door at the far end of the dining room led back into the primary hallway. The hallway was impressive; a towering staircase stood in the center of the room, leading to a large landing spreading across the first floor. Opposite the dining room, on the other side of the staircase, was another door leading into the living room with a large stone fireplace and multiple windows showing the woods outside. Next to the living room was another door leading to an old drawing room which Silas' father had already claimed as his office.

The staircase creaked on every stair, and the handrail felt like it might fall apart any second. The first floor held two large bedrooms, both ensuite. That surprised Silas as the rest of the house seemed so old. Another small staircase led to the third floor (an attic space converted into two smaller bedrooms with ensuite bathrooms). Each bedroom had a small fireplace and two large arch-shaped windows. The room at the front of the house had a dull view of the road leading to the house and the dry dirt path leading back into town.

The bedroom at the back of the house was slightly bigger, with larger closet space and an impressive view of the woods and the stream.

"I think this room is going to be mine," Silas said, snapping several pictures and sending them to his friends.

The excitement of the creepy new house faded rapidly. There was not much else to report to his friends, and the nearest town was a five-mile bike ride away. Silas spent most of the first week curled up in bed on his phone. Even when his father asked him to help with the repairs, Silas was in front of the screen every spare second. He pined for his friends as they uploaded pictures of themselves at the Spring Break Fair and the local arcade.

To distract himself from the sadness in his heart and the loneliness that followed him, Silas took his friend's advice and began documenting the house—the state of disrepair to the moment his father fixed it. He even created spooky stories about fictional people who once called the property home. His followers loved it, temporarily feeding into his need to feel friendship and love. But soon enough, that high faded, leaving Silas alone in his new room with his thoughts.

3

"Silas, come help your mother paint the dining room," his father yelled up the stairs.

Silas didn't answer, too busy scrolling through the online comments on the post of him in the creepy car. The only other place on the property that seemed to bring him the slightest joy.

"Silas! Now!" his father yelled.

Huffing, Silas stomped down the stairs, pushing past his father to the dining room two floors down. His mother told him what walls to paint. Smiling, she passed him a paint roller. By the time his mother had finished painting two walls, she had turned to find Silas sitting on the floor with his face on his phone, having only painted two strips of one wall.

"Silas, if you aren't going to help me, I'm getting rid of that stupid car," his mother snapped.

"What? You can't," Silas protested.

"Then, if you aren't going to help me, help your father. We only have a day before we start our new jobs, and there is a lot still to do around this house. I think your father is weeding the garden. You never know, you might find some treasures," his mother smiled, trying not to sound as angry and frustrated as she felt.

Strolling out to the back of the house, Silas searched for his father. The sound of sheers snapping branches told Silas to venture around the front porch. With a sweat-soaked brow, his father snipped branches and pulled at vines with all his might, trying to tame the chaos of the garden.

"Mom says I should help you," Silas said, his eyes still on his phone.

"Sure, grab the rake and help turn all this debris into a pile. I'll bag it up later and get rid of it then," his father said, jumping right back into hacking at the vines that threatened to take over the porch.

Half-heartedly pulling the rake through the dead grass and leaves, Silas sighed. He wished he was doing anything but helping with mind-numbing chores. Suddenly, the rake caught on something. Silas tugged and tugged, but it wouldn't budge. His curiosity piqued, and Silas pulled his phone out of his back pocket, preparing to capture whatever treasure the vines held.

"Dad! Look what I found!" Silas exclaimed excitedly, pulling an old tire and steering wheel from the creepy car.

"Perfect, son."

"I'll be right back; I'm going to put them with the car," Silas said, grabbing his find and running off.

Snapping pictures of his discovery, Silas uploaded the picture before placing the spare tired in the car's trunk and clipping the steering wheel back on. Next, Silas snapped a selfie in the driver's seat and uploaded the picture with a caption stating, 'Finally complete and in the driver's seat. What time should I travel to first?'

It didn't take long before the likes and comments rolled in, and even less time for Silas to forget what he was doing and spend the rest of the afternoon scrolling through social media in the car.

SILAS KNEW his parents were mad at him at dinner, but he didn't care; he was angry with them too. If they wanted him to be happy, they should have stayed in the city. But no. They ripped him from his friends, school, and life. So, Silas was content with snubbing them and letting them experience what it was like to feel lonely and ignored.

His mother placed his dinner in front of him on the table. He tried ignoring that, too, but he was hungry, and meatloaf was his favorite. Stabbing at his food with one hand and scrolling through his phone with the other, Silas sank into his own little world, deeper into a fantasy land away from his mundane reality.

"Silas?" he heard his father's voice say.

"Huh?" Silas gruffed without looking up from his phone.

"If you don't eat your vegetables, you don't get ice cream for dessert. I picked up your favorite at the store today," his mother said.

"Vegetables, sure," Silas mumbled.

"That's it!" snapped his mother, slamming her hand on the table.

In one quick move, his mother had traveled the table length and snatched his phone from his hand. Then, turning it off, she shoved it into her pocket.

"What the? Mom, give that back!" Silas yelled.

"Silas! Do not talk to your mother with that tone!" yelled his father.

"We have been here for over a week, and you have had your head in that stupid device this entire time. I asked you to help paint, and you didn't. Your father asked to help with the garden, and you ran off to sit in that stupid car with your head on your phone. I'm tired of having a son who never says more than two words. You are part of this family and will start acting like it!" yelled his mother.

Silas was stunned; he had never seen his mother act like that before. She was usually so happy and composed and never raised her voice. Silas had never once heard his parents argue or say a bad word to each other in all his years. Dumbfounded, Silas looked at her wide-eyed, unsure what to say or do.

"Tomorrow, you will act like a normal fourteen-year-old. There are acres of woods around this house; explore, have an adventure. And tomorrow at dinner, I want to hear all about it."

4

WHEN SILAS WOKE the following day, the house was dead silent. He could hear the trees rustling in the breeze and the slow, steady trickle of the stream at the back of the property. Silas rolled over, reaching for his phone, instantly remembering his mother had taken it. Frustrated, he quickly dressed and headed to his parent's room. It was locked. But Silas knew these locks were old and easy to pick. He and his father had to pick a lock or two on the day they moved in.

Silas searched through the dresser and bedside cabinets for his phone. Still, he found nothing but old bills, magazines, his mother's medications, and jewelry. Then, moving onto the closet, he searched high and low, inside shoe boxes and even in his parent's coat pockets. Again, he came up empty.

Heading downstairs, he called to see if his parents were still home, but no one answered. Peeking out the front door, his parent's car was gone. He was alone in a creepy new house in the middle of nowhere with no phone. Determined not to let his mother defeat him, he searched every place he could. Going room to room, he checked cupboards, drawers, and any place that could open; he even checked the fridge in desperation.

Inside was a packed lunch for Silas to enjoy throughout the day. Attached was a pink Post-it note from his mother:

Here is a lunch for you. Take it with you when you explore the grounds. Don't bother looking for your phone. I took it to work with me. See you at dinner. I can't wait to hear about your day. Love, Mom xx

"She took it with her?" Silas yelled, his voice echoing through the empty house.

Silas slammed the fridge door and sat at the dining room table with his face in his hands. That's when the thought came to him. He didn't need his phone to get online. So, taking his trusty pin, he headed to his father's office at the back of the house. To his surprise, the door wasn't locked. Sitting, pride of place, on the desk was his dad's laptop. The computer sprang to life when Silas hit the power button.

Silas ran back to the kitchen in a blaze of excitement, filled his hands with snacks and drinks, and set up camp comfortably in his dad's office. All was going great until a screen popped up requesting a password.

Password? What would Dad use as a password? Silas thought.

He tried his mother's name. Nothing. He tried his name. Nothing. He moved on to birthdays, anniversaries, and even their old dog's name. He had failed so many times that the screen flashed up a warning. One more wrong password and the computer would wipe the hard drive clean.

Silas paced the room, searching his mind for the answer. He couldn't risk making a mistake. His dad would go crazy if he came home and his computer's hard drive was wiped. Silas couldn't think of anything that would work until he sat back at his father's desk, and his eyes fell on the picture frame next to the laptop. It was his dad the day he went to the Red Socks game with Silas' grandfather. Etched in the frame were the words, *The Happiest Day of my Life.*

"That's it!" Silas cheered, fiercely typing in the password.

A wheel started to spin on the screen. Silas was so close he could taste it. How much had he missed in the hours since his mother had taken his phone? What exciting news would be waiting in his inbox? Silas bounced in the chair, waiting as the laptop roared to life.

"Yes!" Silas punched the air, opening a bag of chips and tucking in.

Double tapping the mouse pad, he waited for the browser to load. He hummed his favorite tunes until the browser failed. No Wi-Fi. Running to the phone in the kitchen where the Wi-Fi router was kept, Silas wrote the password on his hand. Running back, he typed away, only to be hit with a blaring sign telling him the password was wrong. Silas ran back, not once but twice, to check he had written it down correctly. That was when he saw it, another pink Post-it note. Picking it up from under the table, he read:

Nice try. I changed the Wi-Fi password. Go! Outside! Love, Mom xx.

"Oh, come on!" Silas yelled, scrunching the note and tossing it across the kitchen.

Finally admitting defeat, Silas picked up his backpack and loaded it with the snack and drinks from his father's office. Rummaging through his parent's room, he found their old Polaroid camera. If he were forced to go outside, he would still document what he could until he could get his phone back. Shoving the camera in his bag, he pulled on his hiking boots and headed out through the back porch.

Strolling through the woods, all Silas could think was how stupid this was. How much fun could he have alone? He missed his friends; at least if they were there, they could swim in the stream or climb the trees. Then his mind wondered, what if he got lost? How would he find his way home? Then, turning his head, he saw the stream; it led right back to the house. If he could find that, he would find his way home.

As he followed the stream deeper into the woods, Silas stopped to take pictures of frogs, birds, and fallen trees. After a while, he found he liked exploring the woods. The deeper he got, the more fun things he saw – An old broken wagon that once most likely pulled grain to market. Names were carved into a tree beside an old bike with faded pink handlebars.

Shoving his pictures into his bag, he looked out into the woods and passed the trees. Then, something in the distance caught his eye. Could it be his most significant find yet? Excited, Silas charged ahead.

5

PUSHING through the thickest trees he had seen on his journey, brushing branches out of his face, it came into view. An old, abandoned cabin. It wasn't as big as his house; it was a small farmhouse-type cottage. Silas assumed it was the old caretakers' cabin. But nature had taken it over, with branches pushing through the windows and cracking the foundation. The hairs on the back of Silas' neck stood on end—a chill took over his body, covering him in goosebumps. Amazed, he snapped a picture. Silas walked around the back and took more pictures, excited to show his friends and growing online following.

The back door was hanging off its hinges; one slight pull and the door came off in his hand. Jumping back just in time to miss being hit by the door, Silas smiled, snapping a picture of the darkened house.

The building was one story with only a few small rooms. The first room Silas entered was the kitchen. Vines from the window took over the countertops and the sink. Debris littered the floor from the hole in the roof, and much of the floor had rotted away. Silas' camera flash lit up the dark room. He jumped. He thought he saw something for a second, only to laugh at himself jumping at his shadow. Moving to the next room, he found an old wooden fireplace with a large black pot hanging over the logs. A decrepit armchair with torn fabric and bite marks from rats sat in the corner. A dusty grandfather clock with its glass smashed, and the pendulum lying on the floor stood against a dark wall. Silas couldn't get enough.

Under the window by the front door was an old dresser. Silas opened every drawer, hoping to find treasures. He didn't find much, a few old coins, a pocketknife, and a once-white cotton handkerchief with the initials C.B. in the bottom corner. Pocketing his finds, he snapped pictures, took a pen from his bag, and made notes on the back of each photograph of caption ideas. His creative juices were flowing, his mind racing as he imagined the life of whoever once called the cabin home. On top of the fireplace was an old smoking pipe. Silas took a photo and reached up to take the pipe.

As soon as his fingers touched the pipe, a loud, sharp bone-chilling scream pierced his ears. Silas dropped the pipe leaving only a silhouette in the dust where it once stood. His heart thundered in his chest, and his hands began to shake. Silas spun, trying to find the location of the scream—suddenly, Silas froze in place.

The door leading to the bedroom was dark. Only a tiny amount of light from the window highlighted the bed in the corner—but that wasn't what scared Silas. In the door frame stood a dark, faceless figure. A shadow took over the frame. Terror raced in Silas' veins, he felt like he couldn't breathe, and his breath froze in the air.

Silas bolted like lightning to the front door, not wanting to find out what, or who, the mystery figure was. Kicking it open, he charged through the woods. His breath came thick and fast as he kept his eyes on the stream leading back to his house.

Don't look back! Don't look back! Silas kept telling himself as the scream followed him home through the woods.

The scream seemed to move with the wind, rustling the leaves in the trees and making the birds take flight. Watching the birds flee only encouraged Silas to run faster. Were those footsteps he could hear behind him? Was he being chased? His parents wouldn't be home for hours; he was alone.

His house finally came into view, but in his terrified state of mind, every step seemed to take him a mile in the other direction. The more desperate he was to get inside and lock the doors, the slower his feet seemed to run. When he was nearly home, Silas tripped over his feet and stumbled just before the back porch steps. Scrambling through the earth, digging his fingers into the ground, he jumped to his feet, taking the steps two at a time. Then, pushing the door open, he charged inside, slamming it shut behind him, turning the key, and locking it tight.

The back door had a large windowpane in the center. Too scared to look back in case something followed, Silas ran through the kitchen, the dining room, and up the stairs. Racing past his parent's bedroom, he flew through the final floor, locking his door tight. He pulled his dresser across his door and jumped under his bed.

Shaking from head to toe, Silas held his hand over his mouth to hide his heavy breathing. Silas couldn't remember a time he had ever felt so scared. A genuine fear like no other. Fear he couldn't put into words. With eyes clenched tightly shut, he listened carefully for every creak and crack the house made. A scratch on the window had Silas curling into a tighter ball. Who – or what – was out there? Was it the tree tapping against his window? Did he hear footsteps coming up the stairs? When would his parents be home?

Silas desperately wanted to call his mom, but she had his phone. The landline was in the kitchen, by the back door. And Silas was determined he was not leaving that room anytime soon. Hours passed as Silas waited under his bed. His mind raced with scenarios of where that scream could have come from, what the figure was in the doorway was, and how it would hunt him down while he slept. He had fallen asleep and the house was silent when he woke. Nothing had followed him, so what was that sound?

"Silas? We are home!" came his mother's cheery voice from the hallway.

6

"I'LL BE RIGHT DOWN," Silas called, crawling from under his bed.

"No rush, darling, I'll call you when dinner is ready," his mother yelled.

Silas sat on his bedroom floor; he had been under his bed for hours. Climbing onto his bed, he peeked out the window, looking towards the woods. Everything seemed normal. Nothing had come to get him; nothing looked disturbed, like a monster had traveled through the woods. He felt foolish.

Sitting on his bed, he opened his backpack and pulled out his pictures. Looking over them, everything seemed normal. An old cabin, lost to time, taken over by nature. No ghouls or goblins, no ghosts, or strange shadows. Silas laughed at himself.

I was so scared, and for what? I'm not a kid anymore, he told himself.

The smell of dinner being prepared reminded Silas that he hadn't eaten all day. He had been so scared he hadn't noticed his hunger before. Silas hurried to the bathroom, took a quick bath, and changed into jeans and a sweatshirt for dinner. Apart from his moment of madness, the expedition into the woods had been quite fun, and he found he couldn't wait to tell his parents all about it.

Silas bounced into the dining room just as his mother served the food.

"Someone seems to be in a chipper mood. Did you have a good day?" his mother asked, kissing him on the forehead as he took his seat.

"I did. I hope you don't mind that I borrowed your old Polaroid camera," Silas said, tucking into his spaghetti.

"The old Polaroid? I'm surprised that thing still works," his father laughed.

"Go on, son, tell us about your day," his mother beamed.

Silas rambled between bites sliding photographs down the table. He gave detailed descriptions of each of the birds and insects. He talked about the stream and how the trees grew in unusual patterns.

"And then I found...." Silas felt himself grow cold once more.

Did he want to tell his parents about the cabin? Would his mother be mad he ventured so far out?

"Fawmd whap?" his father asked with a mouth full of food, earning himself a disapproving look from his wife.

"An old cabin—look," Silas slid the picture across to his father, his hands shaking at the thought.

"Oh yeah, the realtor said this place once had a caretaker. That explains why the grounds are so unruly. No one had tended to the gardens for years," his father laughed, passing the picture to his mother.

"How scary," his mother joked, mockingly shaking her shoulders and widening her eyes.

"I wasn't scared. I'm not scared. I'm a grown boy, not a child," Silas insisted, more for himself than anything.

"I was just teasing, darling," his mother laughed. "What else did you find, my little explorer?"

Silas pulled up his backpack and produced the few treasures he found. His mother and father's conversation slowly drifted to their new jobs. Silas' mind wandered back to the cabin. His eyes fixed on the pictures scattered across the table made him feel more relaxed. Still, he wanted to keep the rest of the details of his encounter with the cabin to himself.

"Mom? Can I have my phone back now?" Silas asked.

"No, darling. You don't need it; look how much fun you had without it. This is the most I have seen you smile since we moved. So, finish unpacking your room and while your father and I are at work tomorrow, take your bike and head into town. Make some new friends, and then I will think about giving you back your phone."

"Come on, Joanna, give the boy back his phone. He has learned his lesson," his father insisted.

His mother's eyes grew firm, and she instantly shot her husband a look that silenced him.

"Yeah, no phone until your mother says so."

Silas couldn't help but laugh, earning a wink and a smile from his mother.

"It's for the best, darling. I know how much you miss your old friends. But before you start school again in the fall, you should use this time to make new friends. How will you make new friends if you fixate on the old ones? But, of course, you won't forget them. They can still come to visit, but you also need friends here," his mother smiled.

Whenever she gave Silas that warm, loving look that melted into puppy dog eyes, Silas couldn't help but feel the love for his mother grow in his heart. He knew she was right, and he knew she meant well. He might have been angry and reluctant initially, but if he considered himself a grown-up, he needed to stop acting like a child.

"You are right, Mom," Silas smiled, heading over to his mother's chair and hugging her tight.

7

SILAS ATE breakfast with his mom and dad the next day before they went to work. They waved him goodbye, and Silas watched as the car vanished from view. He had promised his mother he would go into town and make new friends. But all night, he had thought about the cabin in the woods at the back of his house. Silas had promised his mother, yes, but he had also made a promise to himself. He had vowed to go back and stay at least an hour to prove to himself he had nothing to be scared of.

Silas told himself he could always go into town after getting to the cabin.

Armed with his backpack loaded with snacks and his father's Polaroid camera, Silas took a deep breath and followed the stream back through the woods. When he eventually found the cabin again, he took a while to rack up the courage to go inside. He wandered around the sides, looking into each window to see if he could notice any changes from the day before. There were no footsteps in the dirt. No track in the dust other than his maddened footprints from where he had run.

This time, Silas entered through the front door. Once his foot stepped over the threshold, he clicked the timer on his watch, setting his alarm for an hour. Then, standing in the living room, Silas stood dead still, staring at the door frame to the bedroom. Slowly, he took a step closer, then another, giving him a better view from the inside. Then, finally, he walked straight into the heart of the room.

There was nothing special about the room; if anything, Silas found it disappointing compared to the rest of the house. The window was almost overtaken by the overgrown tree outside the window, allowing only a minute bit of light in through the branches. A torn white cloth hung from the window frame, what remained of a pair of curtains; the other half was lying dirt-covered on the floor.

Under the window lay a single wooden framed bed. Its mattress was torn with springs sticking out at odd angles. The only other piece of furniture in the room was a small chair in the corner. The bedroom might not have been as interesting as everywhere else, but nonetheless, Silas took as many pictures as he could.

Venturing from room to room didn't take long. Silas paced the small cabin until a loud beeping sound made him jump. It had been an hour. Nothing had happened. No screams, no shadows. Everything was fine. Silas laughed loudly, his side hurting from laughing so hard.

I was so stupid. I knew there was nothing to fear. It was all in my imagination. A trick of the light, Silas thought.

On the journey home, Silas admired his pictures and the nature surrounding his home with a new sense of self-confidence. Perhaps he could go into town and make new friends after all.

Silas' bike wasn't anything special, but—for his birthday the previous year—his mother and father bought him the exact same one Jake and Ben had. It meant the world to him to have the same bike as his friends.

Silas' house was five miles away from the nearest town. A long dry, dusty dirt road that once was an old railroad served as the only one-way road connecting all the houses along the five-mile stretch to the town. It was an exciting ride, giving Silas time to think and work up a speech in his head about how he would introduce himself to all the new kids he would meet.

From what Silas could tell, most of the houses nearby were like his – gated off for privacy and a long drive before you reached the property, all hidden by trees so you wouldn't see the houses or even know they were there.

The sun was beaming down, and halfway to the town, Silas was getting thirsty. Pulling off his bag, he pulled out a now-warm water bottle and took a welcome sip. Ahead of him, he could hear the sounds of the town. Car engines, muffled voices, laughter, and machinery reminded Silas of the car repair shop back in the city. A host of smells traveled down the lane, making Silas' stomach grumble. He continued riding back on his bike, imagining the town's stores. He could smell a baker and perhaps butchers as he drew closer, or was he so hungry he imagined he could smell it all?

ARRIVING IN TOWN, Silas was not disappointed. While the town was small and not as bustling with life as he expected, everyone he rode by smiled and waved. Everyone seemed so welcoming and friendly. There indeed were butchers, bakers, and a florist in the town, as well as a bookstore, a grocery store, a bar, and a library. In the middle of town stood a sizeable two-story water fountain surrounded by a beautiful plush garden of roses, violets, and lilies.

As Silas rode closer to the fountain, he noticed four, maybe five, bikes like his leaning up against the fountain. Following the sound of laughter over the fountain's rushing water, Silas saw a group of boys. Some were on skateboards, and some were on roller skates. The boys were roughly Silas' age, but a few looked a year or two older. They laughed at each other and taught each other tricks. Silas stopped and watched for a while, hidden by a large bush on the garden's edge.

Hi, I'm Silas. I'm new in town, can I be your friend? No, that's lame, Silas cursed himself. *Hi, I'm new in town. Can I hang with you guys? Wow, that looks so cool. Can you teach me?*

The longer Silas watched and the sillier the introductions he came up with, the more his stomach turned. These boys were nothing like his friends back home, and there were a lot of them. Perhaps he might have ventured to say hello if there were just two or three. But with a sinking heart and a new wave of loneliness combined with homesickness, Silas turned and began to peddle back out of town to the new house he still couldn't call home.

Just as Silas reached the edge of town, about to join the long dusty dry dirt road that would be a lonely and trying five-mile bike ride, he heard a bell. A sweet metal tinkle pulled him to a stop. Looking over his shoulder, he saw an odd-looking girl.

Her bike looked old and worn, in shades of brown and cream. She wore a simple white dress past her knee with white and yellow sunflowers around the trim. Her hair was golden like the sun and tied in two braids that fell over her shoulders. Her face was covered in freckles that spanned her nose. And her hands were covered in white lace gloves.

Silas looked surprised as the girl waved at him, a small but stiff gesture. Slowly Silas smiled and waved back, waiting for the girl to catch up on her bike.

"Hi, I'm Cassandra. What's your name?" asked the girl.

On closer inspection, Silas realized she was quite pretty. She had a small, round button nose, deep green eyes, and a petite slim mouth with high cheekbones that grew red like apples when she smiled.

"I'm Silas; I'm new to town," Silas smiled back.

"I thought you might be. I haven't seen you around here before," Cassandra chuckled.

"Yeah, my parents and I moved here a little over a week ago. I live just up the dirt road, at the top," Silas pointed towards home.

"Oh my goodness, so do I. Do you want to ride home together?" Cassandra asked excitedly.

"Sure, why not?" Silas smiled.

As they rode down the dirt road, they talked about how odd they thought the other was.

Cassandra remarked on Silas' bizarre name and strange accent, and Silas commented on her old-looking bike and old lady clothes. Neither took offense, laughing each comment off.

"Shall we meet at the end of the lane tomorrow and ride back into town together?" Cassandra asked.

"I'd like that," Silas smiled.

They rode a little further before Silas stopped to say he was home. When he turned around, Cassandra was gone.

Oh, that's why she asked to meet tomorrow. Oh man, I was so rude not even saying goodbye. I hope she doesn't mind, Silas thought as he pushed his gates open and rode up to the house.

8

THE NEXT DAY when Silas took his bike down the dirt road to town, he was pleased to see Cassandra waiting exactly where they had arranged to meet. But, after she vanished on their bike ride home, Silas worried that his friendship was a prank or a cruel trick cooked up by the boys in town.

"Morning, Silas. What shall we do today?" Cassandra asked with a smile.

"Well, you know this town better than me. Want to show me around?"

"Of course, follow me."

Cassandra and Silas spent the day biking around town. First, Cassandra showed Silas the lake surrounding the town from her favorite spot on top of the hills, which gave a perfect view of the town below. Then, they went to the bakery to buy cookies and cake and exchanged stories at the fountain in the town square. Silas liked Cassandra; she was intelligent and funny and told the strangest anecdotes. They intrigued and excited Silas. Silas had almost forgotten about not having his phone, social media, or old friends back in the city. They explored and talked for so long that the sun had begun to set before they knew it.

"Oh no, I better get home before my parents start to worry. They will be home from work already," Silas explained.

"Shall we meet again tomorrow?" Cassandra asked.

"Sure," Silas smiled.

Cassandra and Silas met at the end of the lane every day for the rest of the week. On the second day, they traveled to the lake at the far end of town. It was a gloriously sunny day, and they wanted to keep cool. Silas had packed a picnic for them to enjoy after their swim. Cassandra was a great swimmer; Silas needed a bit of practice, he didn't swim much in the city, and Cassandra laughed the few times he struggled and almost drowned.

The next day, they went to the library and read other passages from their favorite books. Silas was only told to shush twice by the angry-looking librarian.

"I can't believe you have never seen a comic book before," Silas whispered, closely watching the librarian.

One more outburst, and Silas knew they would be kicked out.

"I have...I've just never seen this one. It's so strange. I love it. It's so bright and colorful, and the idea of a man who can fly is astounding," Cassandra cheered.

"This town really is in the middle of nowhere if you have never heard of Superman before," Silas joked.

"Silas, what time do you think it is? Your father and I were worried you had gotten lost," his mother panicked, hugging him tightly as he arrived home.

"Sorry, I got caught up with Cassandra. Before we knew it, the day had gotten away from us," Silas answered.

"Who's Cassandra?" his father asked with a mischievous grin.

"My new friend. She's so cool. She dresses weird and talks a bit oddly, like an old lady. Like Grandma, but she's cool. She showed me all around town, and we biked home together. She lives round here too," Silas chirped, excited to talk about his new friend.

"That's lovely, darling; I'm glad you're making friends."

"I guess you don't need your phone all the time after all," his father said with a wink.

For the rest of the week, over dinner, all Silas could talk about was Cassandra and the adventures they had that day. They quickly became close friends.

"You should have her come to dinner one night," Silas' mother offered.

"I would, but her father is rigorous—she has to be home before dark and isn't allowed out after. I think he is in the police force or something. She mentioned something about him being an officer. That's also why I haven't visited her house yet. She isn't allowed to have friends over unless her parents are home," Silas answered.

"That's smart. I like the sound of her father. I agree on not allowing friends around when home alone."

"Maybe one night we could invite her parents round too?" Silas asked.

"Wow, you must really like this girl," his father chirped.

"Dad, she's my friend," Silas blushed.

9

SILAS SLEPT PEACEFULLY in his bed, warmly wrapped in his thick blanket. He dreamed about the adventures he and Cassandra had planned for the next day and about introducing her to Louise, Caroline, Jake, and Ben when they finally came to visit. Silas was happy, content, and looking forward to starting school in the fall for the first time since moving to Golden-Vale.

His peaceful dream state was suddenly disturbed by the same bone-chilling scream he heard when he discovered the cabin. Sitting bolt upright, Silas panted, pressing his hand to his chest. He felt his heart racing. Then, feeling braver than before, he peeked out his window. It was too dark to see if anything was out of the ordinary.

Silas could still hear his father's loud snoring from the floor below. How had his parents slept through that? Had they heard it? Curious, Silas snuck down outside his parent's room. Sneaking a peek, he saw they were still sound asleep.

With Dad's snoring and Mom's earplugs, it made sense that they didn't hear, Silas told himself.

Curious and surprisingly not scared, Silas decided to continue being brave. At least he would have another fun story to add to his collection and something fun to tell Cassandra in the morning. He quickly dressed, grabbed a flashlight and his camera, and crept downstairs as quietly as possible.

Sneaking out the back porch, Silas followed the stream up to the cabin. Silas' walk through the woods at night was scarier than tracking down a mystery screaming monster in an abandoned house. The woods seemed alive. Crickets chirped. Owls hooted. Every rustle in the bushes and snap of a branch had Silas jumping. But he was on a mission and wasn't heading home until he checked the cabin.

Finally, the cabin appeared; it was creepier at night. The window whistled through the building, but aside from that, when Silas investigated, everything was normal. He hadn't heard another scream since he left his room. The cabin was exactly how he left it. Confused and slightly disappointed, Silas headed home.

Silas couldn't understand how his parents hadn't woken up. Had he been the only one to hear the scream? Cassandra lived nearby. Silas wondered if she had heard it too. He planned on asking her in the morning and hoped she hadn't ventured out to search like he had.

"I'M off to meet Cassandra. Have a good day at work," Silas called to his parents.

"Silas, wait. Here is your phone back," smiled his mother.

"Thanks, Mom. See you later."

Silas waited at the end of the lane for half an hour. There was no sign of Cassandra. He waited a little longer, but there was still no sign.

Maybe she decided to ride into town, Silas thought.

Silas rode around town looking, but still no luck. He checked all their favorite places: the lake, bakery, fountain, and library. Eventually, Silas gave up and headed home. Silas felt foolish; he had never once offered to walk her home, so he didn't know where she lived. And even without his cell, he never asked for her landline number.

So, he had no way of getting in touch with her. A strange twisting in his stomach told him something was wrong, and he hoped she was okay.

Three days passed, and Silas still hadn't seen Cassandra. Concerned, he decided to ride back into town and ask if anyone had seen her. He started at the lake. Groups of kids of all ages swam, danced to music from their boomboxes, and ate on picnic blankets.

Cassandra would love this, Silas thought.

"Hi guys, have you seen Cassandra...oh shoot, I don't know her last name. She's a bit odd, blonde, and rides an old rusty bike. You have probably seen her with me around town," Silas asked a group of boys on skateboards.

"I don't know anyone in this town called Cassandra," one boy replied.

"Well, she lives up the dirt road like me," Silas said.

"Dude, it's a small town. Even if you live miles away, everyone knows everyone in this town," mocked another.

Silas walked further down the bank, asking a group of girls and a small family. He mentioned her father was an officer, hoping one of the adults would know him, but no one did. Confused and more worried than ever, he headed to the bakery.

"Hi Mrs. Jackson, have you seen Cassandra? I haven't seen her for a few days, and I'm starting to worry. No one else seems to know her either. It's weird."

"Cassandra? Who's Cassandra?" asked Mrs. Jackson as she served another customer.

"The girl I've been biking around town with. We came in earlier in the week. You must remember," Silas insisted.

"Sorry, sugar. I don't remember seeing you with anyone. But to be honest, I was worried about you."

"Why?" Silas asked.

"Well, there are many kids in this town, but you are always alone," Mrs. Jackson answered, rushing off to stop the alarm on the cake oven, letting her know the next batch of cupcakes were ready.

Silas tried the fountain, the bookstore, and the police station, even more confused than ever. Everyone looked at him like he had gone mad. No one knew of a Cassandra, and none of the officers in the station had a daughter, sister, or niece called Cassandra either.

"It's so sad. These big-city kids always have trouble adjusting to small-town life. He has convinced himself his imaginary friend is real," Silas overheard the florist say to one of her customers.

Imaginary friend? Why do they think that?

Silas felt frustrated, almost like he could cry. He worried for Cassandra. He feared that no one knew her and hated how everyone assumed he was crazy. Something was wrong.

10

SILAS HAD NEVER BEEN A QUITTER and was determined not to go home until he found someone who knew Cassandra. He thought over their week-long friendship and decided his last chance was the library. The old angry librarian had told them to be quiet a few times. She had to know who Cassandra was. She would have a record of her library card, address, and phone number.

Excitement shot through him, making his skin break out into goosebumps. Then, finally, Silas felt relaxed, relieved, and hopeful. Answers were just a short bike ride away. The day had been crazy enough, not that he was close to getting answers. But he also couldn't wait to tell his parents about his bizarre day.

The library was practically empty. Most kids were at the lake because it was the hottest day of the year. The angry old librarian sat behind the desk reading. She hadn't even noticed Silas come in. Silas quietly wandered around the library, checking all the different sections where he and Cassandra had spent their days together. Silas had hoped he would find her reading one of her favorite old-time books or being amazed at the comic book sections, but she wasn't in the library either.

"Excuse me," Silas whispered, tapping his fingers gently on the desk in front of the librarian.

Elegantly closing her book and peeking over her half-moon glasses, the librarian finally looked at Silas.

"Oh, the noisy boy from the other day. How can I help you?"

"I'm scared. I can't find my friend. I've searched the entire town and asked everyone, but they all look at me like I'm crazy. I'm not crazy. It's been three days," Silas panicked.

"I'm sorry, but I can't help you. Have you tried the police station?" the librarian asked.

She came from behind her desk and began pushing a trolly of books that needed to be restacked. She was trying to avoid talking to Silas, but Silas wasn't going to give up that easily. The librarian was his last hope.

"I've tried the police station and was told to stop wasting police time. The florist even suggested I had an imaginary friend, but I don't. You have seen me with her."

"Seen you with who?"

"Cassandra, my friend. You told us to be quiet when we were laughing the other day."

The librarian stopped in her tracks, placing a hand on her hip. She turned and looked Silas up and down. Then, rolling her eyes, she sighed and reshelved the books.

"I have no idea what you are talking about. You were alone last time you were here. I thought you were rude and a bit strange. Sitting talking to yourself like that."

"What? I wasn't alone. She was here with me," Silas insisted.

"I don't know what to tell you, little man. I have only ever seen you alone. Now, if you will excuse me, I have work to do."

Silas stopped, frozen in place. Then, starting to get annoyed that no one was taking him seriously, he ran in front of the librarian's trolly and forced her to stop and listen.

"You *have* to remember seeing her with me. She is blonde with bangs and long braids. She had freckles across her cheeks and nose..."

As Silas continued to describe Cassandra in as much detail as possible, the librarian's eyes grew wide.

Slowly, she removed her glasses and clenched at her pearl necklace. She seemed to be frightened. Her breath came in small, short pants. All color drained from her cheeks, and she shivered as if a cold breeze had washed over her.

"What did you say her name was?"

"Cassandra," answered Silas.

The librarian looked over her shoulder, checking how busy the library was, before gently grabbing Silas' hand and leading him to the back of the building and the old microfiche viewer. The machine took a while to come to life. It looked like it hadn't been used for years, with a thick layer of dust.

Silas watched nervously while the librarian began flicking through old newspapers. Headlines flashed in front of his eyes, and she flicked further back. Finally, she stopped at a picture of a young girl smiling in front of a house, holding her new bike. Behind her stood a man in an army uniform with a smoking pipe clenched in his teeth.

"Is that her?" the librarian asked, pointing at the screen.

"Yes. But I don't understand," Silas gasped.

The house in the picture was his house. It was undeniable; just off the porch was the car, but it looked brand new. The photo was dated *1922*. It was one hundred years old.

"I can't believe it," gasped the Librarian.

"That's my house. Who is she? What's going on?" Silas panicked.

"She was the general's daughter. She was admitted to a mental asylum when she started acting strange."

"Strange how?" Silas asked.

"What's your name?"

"My name? Silas Jones, why?" Silas answered.

"Oh, good heavens," The librarian panicked, fanning herself with her hand.

"What's wrong?" Silas asked.

"Read it."

Scared, Silas turned back to the screen and began to read. Suddenly, the air around him grew cold. His heart pounded in his chest, and his hands trembled. He couldn't believe what he was reading.

The article told the heartbreaking story of the general's daughter, who one day began acting strange. She was found interacting with an invisible boy claiming he was from the future. Her mother had begged her father not to have her committed, but the general was a harsh man and dragged her from her room. Cassandra had begged and pleaded for her father to believe her. She told her father of the books the boy had shown her of a man who could fly and wore a red cape. She tried to prove herself by describing the boy who had recently moved to town from the big city. But nothing she said could convince her father she was sane. As the asylum staff dragged her from her home, she screamed so loud it could be heard across town. The last words of the article caused Silas to jump back in fear. Cassandra's last words before her father had her admitted to the asylum.

"Silas Jones. His name is Silas Jones!"

The End.

CRANKED

1

IT WAS that time of year again. Gordon, the lighthouse keeper, was due to take his two-week vacation like he had done every summer for the past thirty years. This year, he planned to go upstate to visit his daughter. She had just given birth to Gordon's fifth grandchild, a beautiful little boy named John.

Gordon may look forward to his vacation every year, but the rest of the small seaside town did not. With the lighthouse keeper off on his annual travels, someone from the town would have to man the lighthouse.

The lighthouse had a history—a history of changing anyone who entered. Previous volunteers had vanished, died, or never been the same again. So, when the butcher's son returned after his two-week stint in the lighthouse as white as a ghost and unable to form a sentence, everyone knew something was wrong. When weeks turned to months, and the poor boy still jumped at his own shadow and suffered from violent night terrors, the other town folk swiftly stopped volunteering.

The town's livelihood relied on the ships. They sailed in with produce. And tourists sailed in on river cruises to explore the town's rich history. For the town to survive, someone had to man the lighthouse for those two weeks. Rumors spread like wildfire that Gordon knew of the strange things that happened over the two weeks in summer, and that's why he left. Other rumors spread that Gordon was murdering the volunteers. And if he couldn't kill them, he scared them half to death. The stories flew around and seemed crazier and more far-fetched than the last. But one thing for sure was that no one wanted to volunteer.

"Here ye, here ye, all gather round!" yelled the town crier. He was prepared to read the mayor's notice.

A small crowd was gathering to listen to the news.

"It is that time of year again where one volunteer must man the lighthouse. This year, the mayor is offering a salary of five hundred dollars to entice volunteers. To sign up, please head to the mayor's office. Volunteer applications close Friday!" the crier called as he rang his bell.

The crowd groaned and carried on with their daily lives. No amount of money seemed to be enough. By the end of the week, when no one had signed up, the mayor sent out another message offering to increase the pay to eight hundred dollars. But still, no one accepted the job. Finally, the mayor grew tired and called a town meeting.

"As no one seems to want to volunteer to man the lighthouse from here on out, I shall be holding a lottery. One name shall be pulled randomly from the hat, and that person shall man the lighthouse until Gordon comes back from his vacation," said the mayor.

"What? You can't force us!" protested the townsfolk.

"What choice do I have? Summer is our busiest time of year. If we neglect the lighthouse, our small town will crumble. Our economy needs that lighthouse. I have offered a very generous salary for a two-week vacancy, but that doesn't seem to work. So, a lottery shall be enforced. If you do not wish to be involved, you are welcome to leave the town. No vacations are permitted during those two weeks of summer to avoid runaways. Those are the rules."

From that moment on, the Lighthouse lottery was born.

"What happens when Gordon retires? Who will take over the lighthouse full-time then?"

"I bet the mayor will hold a lottery for that too."

The banker's daughter, Kate, was the first name drawn. She had just turned eighteen and was due to leave for college in the fall. She begged her father to exchange places and demanded a redraw, but no one stepped forward.

When she emerged from the lighthouse two weeks later, she didn't speak for weeks. She wouldn't eat and was a shell of her former self. By the end of summer, she had crept up to the cliff's edge and leaped into the sea, never to be seen again.

Earl, the owner of the town's fishing fleet, was called the year after. He went in but never came out.

It had been almost two decades since the lottery was formed that anyone had last volunteered. The mayor had created the lottery to save the town's sea trade. But as the years flew by, more and more people left town. No one wanted to be involved in the lottery; the fear of their name being pulled was almost as bad as the fear of the old lighthouse itself.

As a way to try and keep people in town and encourage them to volunteer, the mayor offered a one-thousand-dollar paycheck to whoever volunteered, free food delivered, and a small house on the edge of town – the house would only go to a volunteer. Yet it still wasn't enough.

2

JAKE and his father had just moved to town. An opportunity to be the lead on a tuna boat came up with a salary double what Jake's dad was used to. A boat was included, as well as a three-bedroom house. It was hard for Jake's dad to refuse the role.

Jake wasn't happy about moving to the middle of nowhere in a stinky fishing town. But until he had enough money to get his own place and car fixed, he had to go wherever his father went.

Jake's dad had always insisted that Jake follow in his footsteps and become a fisherman. But Jake hated fish and hated the sea even more. Surfing the waves or going for a quick swim was fun, but boats were one thing Jake couldn't stomach. It was a subject that Jake and his father fought over a lot.

"If you are not planning on being a fisherman like me, your grandfather, and his father before him, what do you intend to do? Huh?" Jake's dad argued.

"I don't know, Dad. But I don't want to be a fisherman. The money sucks, and its stinks, quite literally. I want more from my life. I want to travel and not worry about bills," Jake argued.

"Ha! And how are you going to do that with no job? No money and no plan?"

"I'll figure it out, Dad, but all I know is I'm not being a stupid fisherman!"

Jake stormed off, leaving their little shack on the hill, and headed to the café in town. His dad called out after him, but Jake wasn't listening. He had heard the same argument for years since his mother had left and his older sister had moved to Chicago. He was tired of having the same discussion and all his father's expectations on his shoulders.

One thing that Jake couldn't deny was that while his father angered him, he had a point. Jake needed a plan for the future and at least his first job to start building up his resume. So, grabbing a newspaper and ordering a coffee, he sat in the corner of the café, hidden away from the world, alone with his thoughts.

Taking a pen, he circled job after job and college course after college course to refer back to, but nothing jumped out at him quite like the answer to all his prayers. A small ad was placed in the paper offering one thousand dollars for two weeks' work, accommodation, food, and even a house at the end of the vacancy. Jake read the ad four or five times to ensure he got it right. All he had to do was man the lighthouse on top of the cliff. Pulling out his cell phone from his pocket, he called the number on the ad.

"Good afternoon, the mayor's office. Rachel speaking, how can I help?" came a sweet voice.

"Hi, my name is Jake. I'm calling about the lighthouse vacancy advertised in the county paper."

"Seriously?....hold please while I transfer you."

Jake couldn't believe his luck. The ad wasn't a prank; it seemed too good to be true. So, he arranged to meet the mayor to look over where he would stay and confirm the final details.

The next day, Jake met the mayor. The lighthouse stood right on the cliff edge; the view was incredible. The room he would be staying in was on the ground floor, a small room just big enough for a single bed, a small desk, and a single chair. The job would be simple enough, and he could surf at the beach when he wasn't working.

"I just need to confirm a few things. How old are you?" asked the mayor.

"Seventeen, sir."

The mayor nodded. "Are you sure you want to take this job?"

"Are you kidding? I can surf through the day and stream my favorite shows and movies at night: free food, great pay, and my own house at the end of it. I have no one telling me what I can and can't do and no younger siblings to watch, and I get one thousand dollars for two weeks' work. I'd do this job full-time if I could. What's not to love?"

"You are not from around here, are you? Anyway. You start Monday."

"WHERE ARE YOU GOING?" demanded Jake's father, blocking the doorway.

"I've got a job; accommodations included," Jake answered, tossing his things into this suitcase.

"Where?"

"The lighthouse," Jake answered.

His father folded his arms and glared down at Jake. Jake knew his father was angry. But, with Jake gone, who would he push around? Who would do the chores and look after his younger sisters, who never seemed to want to do anything but make a mess?

"Who will look after the house when I'm at work? Who is going to look after your sisters?"

"Karla is sixteen, and Sam is Thirteen. Dad, they can look after themselves. You wanted me to get a job; you can't be mad that I went and got one," Jake snapped.

Jake realized his father had nothing to say for the first time in his life. Jake had spoken the truth. He had taken his father's advice and used it against him. Besides, what other seventeen-year-old came across an opportunity like this? Jake would be crazy not to go for it.

3

JAKE ARRIVED at the lighthouse just after daybreak. Gordon, the lighthouse keeper, was leaning against the wall smoking a pipe and waiting for Jake's arrival. The lighthouse was framed by the sun's rays over the horizon. It gave the lighthouse a glow, telling Jake he had made the right choice.

The lighthouse looked somewhat different in the morning light – A tall white building with a red roof, with a small one-room building built into the side where Jake could sleep. The bank the lighthouse sat on gave a beautiful view of the sea and the beach below. Jake grew more and more excited with each passing second.

Gordon was an older gentleman with a head of thick, white hair and a beard that could have passed for a Santa beard. Standing in a long blue waterproof coat, Gordon eyed Jake carefully, looking at the lighthouse's next victim.

"Hi, I'm Jake. You must be Gordon," Jake smiled, sticking out his hand for Gordon to shake.

Gordon looked at Jake's outstretched hand and laughed. Then, shaking his head, he emptied the contents of his pipe on the floor, crushing it with his boot before beckoning Jake to follow him inside.

"Leave your suitcase here. You don't want to be lugging it up all the stairs," Gordon groaned, pointing to the single rickety metal bed frame.

The only other door in the small building led directly into the lighthouse. The temperature dropped inside the tall white stone building, giving the bones an odd and unsettling chill. Two rusted metal staircases spiraled the inside of the building. One led to the top of the building, and the other led to what once was a basement space.

The staircase to the basement was dark; Gordon pulled a flashlight from his pocket, lighting the way. The cellar was tiny and held only an electrical board behind a metal cage.

"This is the circuit breakers. If the lighthouse shuts down, you have two things to do. Check here first. If it's the circuit, push these two buttons. If these levers are not down, then it's not the circuit. Come, follow me. I shall show you the crank," Gordon groaned, turning and heading back upstairs.

Behind a sizeable creaky metal door, a rusted lever on a round spinning top connected to several wires was on the second floor.

"This is the crank. If the circuit isn't the problem, then it's the crank. So, you grab this handle, turn it counterclockwise twice, and then continue to turn it clockwise until that light flashes orange. That light tells you that enough power has been generated to power the light."

"Great, got it," Jake grinned.

"I hope you are strong; sometimes it needs to be cranked all day," Gordon chuckled when he saw Jake's shocked expression.

"Follow me; I'll show you where we keep the bulbs. It's recently been changed so you shouldn't need to do it again, but I'll show you anyway.

After Gordon showed Jake the room holding the large round bulbs and explained how to change the bulbs, he took Jake to the final floor. The light was off but still spun. The view was terrific. It stretched so far that it made Jake feel like the lighthouse was the only place on earth. From the top of the lighthouse, he could see the jagged rocks scattered around the bay for at least two miles. The waves were calm enough that time in the morning, and Jake could see two early morning swimmers climbing the rocks and diving into the sea.

"The lighthouse pretty much runs itself. You can press the button by your bed at sunset, which will automatically turn on the light. An alarm will sound if it doesn't come on or there is anything wrong with the circuit. To turn it off, pull the string by the staircase and investigate. Apart from that, you are all set. Any questions?" Gordon asked, grabbing his bag and heading out the door.

"I don't think so. It seems pretty simple," Jake smiled.

"It is. There is only one rule. It is pretty obvious, and if you can't understand it, you are in the wrong job. The light MUST be in from dusk till dawn. The lighthouse is vital in ensuring the ships and boats pass by the bay safely."

"I got that," Jake chuckled.

"Great. Here are the keys. Good luck. I'll see you in two weeks."

Jake stood at the door to his new temporary home and watched as Gordon rushed off down the hill to his big yellow pickup truck. Gordon tossed his case in the back and sped off in a cloud of dust.

The sound of the sea crashing against the rocks, the sea birds singing their morning song, the gentle growing warmth of the sun caressing his skin, and the salty sea smell took over his senses. Taking a deep breath, the air felt cleaner and tasted different this close to the sea. But what Jake felt most was the sense of freedom. For the next two weeks, he was getting a glimpse at life away from his father.

Unpacking his case, he folded his clothes into the small drawers of the desk. He stacked his shoes against the door frame and set his laptop up, giving himself the perfect view from the bed. Jake loaded up the latest episode of Breaking Bad. He knew he was behind the times; everyone had finished watching the show years ago. But Jake never followed the latest trends and never believed the hype. But it was one show he wished he had started earlier. Starting season four, Jake waited for his first food delivery before he decided to go exploring the town.

Three quick blasts against the door, and Jake was off the bed and across the room. But, to his surprise, the food was waiting on the doorstep, and the food delivery girl was charging back down the hill towards her car.

"Strange, not even a hello," Jake shrugged.

Packing his food in the small refrigerator under the desk, Jake locked up and headed down to the bay. On his travels, he found a café, a beach shop selling everything tourists could want and need, a beach rental shop renting jet ski boats and surfboards, and a small tavern connected to the town's B&B.

Further down the bay were the docks. Curiosity pulled at Jake. He wanted to see where his dad would be working. Standing hidden by a docked boat, Jake caught a glimpse of his dad, hard at work, preparing the boat for their next voyage. Even when he was busy at work with no one nearby, his father still had that angry-at-the-world look on his face. Jake wondered if he should stop and say hello until he watched his father snap at a young boat hand.

Shaking his head and deciding not to let his father bring down his mood, Jake headed back to the lighthouse.

4

_____

THE FIRST FEW days went like a breeze. Jake couldn't believe his luck; one day, he just sat in bed listening to music and shopped online for things to put in his new house. He wrote up plans on how to live his best life, prove his father wrong, and even looked into some colleges nearby. With a newfound spring in his step, hope in his heart, and a zest for life, Jake was ready to take on everything life could throw at him.

This is a breeze. I can't believe no one else applied. I could do this all the time; Jake thought as he rested back in bed with his hands behind his head.

The next day, when Jake woke, he ran up and down the lighthouse checking everything was running perfectly again. When he reached the top, he turned off the light for the day and looked out over the stunning sea view. The sun's rays danced on the waves giving the look of diamonds. Seabirds soared high in the sky. And even through the thick glass of the lighthouse, Jake could feel the sun's warmth on his skin. Having spent three days indoors, he decided to take advantage of the glorious summer weather and head to the beach.

Jake remembered the small rental shack and headed there first, renting out a wet suit and a surfboard. Riding the waves gave Jake a further sense of freedom. It was almost overwhelming, and he wanted to recreate that feeling again and again. He surfed until his legs and shoulders ached, and the sun's warmth turned into a soft, gentle summer night breeze. Jake slept better that night than he had in years.

Taking a stroll down the beach again the following day, Jake was pleased to see how many people had come out to enjoy the sun, sea, and sand. Some groups had set up picnics, and others smoked burgers and hot dogs on miniature barbecues. The smells and sounds overtook Jake, filling him with joy. He felt goosebumps.

"Renting a surfboard again today?" asked the kiosk attendant. The man barely faced Jake, looking more to the water, but managed eye contact.

"Yeah, I might even rent out the jet ski later," Jake smiled back.

Jake watched as the other surfers tried to tackle one particularly tricky wave. The water barreled and traveled at speed, knocking the youngsters off their boards and making their friends laugh. Jake studied the tide for a while before deciding he could take it on. He watched how the more experienced surfers held themselves on the board and moved just before falling. He used his observations to complete the barrel successfully. The crowds on the beach who were watching cheered and clapped, making Jake walk with his head held a little higher.

"Hi, you are a really good surfer. I saw you here yesterday too, so cool," smiled a cute redheaded girl playing with her curls.

She eyed Jake head to toe, flirting with him over her sunglasses. Her eyes were like water.

"Thanks. I'm Jake; what's your name?"

"Laura. These are my friends, Kate and Becky," Laura said, pointing to her two friends, who giggled and blushed when Jake waved.

"Are you new in town or just visiting for the summer?" Kate asked.

Jake sat with the girls on their beach towels and joined them for a snack, music, and soda picnic. He explained how his dad had been forced to move here for a better job on the tuna boats and how he was looking to get his own place soon. The girls hung on to Jake's every word. They told him about their different colleges, where Becky studied beauty, Kate studied criminal science, and Laura studied marine biology. Laura spoke of her love of killer whales and how they were sadly endangered.

"So, do you go to school?" Kate asked.

"Not yet. I'm trying to find the right college for me. Still don't know what I want to study, but I like music and movies, so I was thinking about something in producing. Right now, I have a nice little job to tide me over for the next few weeks," Jake beamed.

"Wow, that's so cool. He is cute, funny, has a job, and is getting his own place at seventeen. If you had a car, we would all be fighting over you," Becky joked, her cheeks turning pink as she blushed.

"Yeah, I'm the whole package," Jake laughed. He turned red as well.

"So, where do you work?" Kate asked, finishing off her chicken salad sandwich.

"The lighthouse."

Suddenly, the atmosphere changed. The girls looked at Jake like he had just told them he kidnapped puppies for a living. They slowly backed away from him, eyeing each other, looking for what to say and wondering if they should go.

"What's wrong?" Jake asked.

"Did your name get pulled in the lottery?" Laura asked, her eyes looking sad.

"Lottery? Yeah, I guess you could say that. One thousand dollars for two weeks of work, free food, accommodation, and at the end of it, I get my own little house," Jake laughed.

The girls didn't laugh back. Instead, they sat with somber expressions, clinging to each other like they had seen a ghost. Laura reached out to Kate in a meaningless, halfway gesture to get her attention.

"To be honest, I'm surprised I was the only applicant. The job is easy," Jake said, popping some chips in his mouth.

"Wait. You volunteered?" Kate gasped.

"Yeah. What's the big deal?" Jake asked, starting to feel a bit concerned.

"It was nice meeting you, Jake," Laura sighed.

The girls quickly packed their things and headed up the beach without another word or glancing back at Jake. Dumbfounded, Jake watched them leave but then shrugged his concern away.

Stuck up rich girls. Always looking at the working class as beneath them, Jake thought as he returned the board and headed back to the lighthouse.

Jake spent the next two days inside catching up on his favorite shows and gaming on his laptop. He hadn't given the girls at the beach, or their odd behavior, a second thought, once again feeling grateful for finding such a cushy job.

5

___

FOUR DAYS IN, Jake knew the easygoing nature of his job had to end sometime. It had been far too easy thus far. Jake had just drifted off to sleep when the alarm echoed around his room. Jake fell out of bed with his heart pounding. The alarm was much louder than needed, and the high-pitched screech stung his ears.

"Well, there is no sleeping through that alarm," Jake yelled.

Swiftly remembering Gordon's instructions, Jake threw on his boots, grabbed a flashlight, and headed down to the cellar. After inspecting the circuit, he realized that the issue was with the crank. Heading upstairs, he turned the lever twice anti-clockwise and then continued to turn the crank clockwise until the orange light indicated enough power had been saved, and he was safe. Just to be safe, Jake headed to the top to check if the light was still spinning. Then, with everything working as it should be, Jake headed back to bed.

The next night, the alarm screeched again and the same again the night after. By the end of the first week, Jake had settled into a routine of running up the stairs to turn the crank; each night, he turned it for longer than the night before. His shoulders began to ache from the strain. One night, every time Jake thought everything was okay and he settled back into bed, the alarm would sound again. Jake ran up the stairs three times to man the crank before eventually drifting off to sleep.

But sleep didn't come easy. Jake thought the job would be easy. And for the most part, it was. But easy job or not, Jake was a man of his word and took his responsibilities seriously. The thought of what could happen if the lighthouse wasn't operating smoothly played tricks on his mind, and slowly, the nightmares began.

Jake woke to the sound of fists hammering on the door. When he opened the door, it was no longer the bright summer. The town was dark, and a storm raged from above. A faceless policeman stood at his door, ready to arrest Jake.

"Wait! What have I done?" Jake cried.

"By not doing your job, people have died. Look," the policeman insisted, shoving Jake to the cliff's edge.

Thunder boomed in the clouds, and a bright flash of lightning lit up the rocks at the bottom of the cliff, revealing the horrors below. A tourist ship had crashed. It lay destroyed in the bay, and limp, lifeless bodies floated in the water. Some were bloated, and their mouth's were wide open, while others lay in strange contortions on the rocks. The sea was a deep, almost grainy red. Its waves were foaming and leaping about like many animals fighting. The water ran over the corpses and then receded. He could see one woman floating face-up as a wave overtook her; her head turned and one eye closed.

Jake jumped up, gasping for breath. The cabin was cold, but Jake's bed was soaked with sweat. It took a minute for Jake to realize he had had a nightmare. A nightmare that felt so real he could smell the blood of the dead thick on the air. His head thundered in his ears, and just to be sure, Jake ran to the top of the lighthouse to ensure the light was still on.

The nightmares didn't stop there, either. Every night after that, when Jake would crank the level before bed, Jake had another bad dream. Each dream was more terrifying than the last, each one more detailed and becoming harder and harder to wake up from.

Gordon knocked on the door at the end of the two weeks. Jake explained how everything had gone swimmingly, and there was no news to report. But Gordon looked back at him, angry.

"Everything's fine, huh? What about the fishing boat that got lost at sea?" he grimaced. "They were due to return last night but didn't. A search party has traced their route, and there is no trace of them."

"What fishing boat?" Jake panicked.

Gordon handed Jake the local newspaper. Jake's entire body felt like he was being submerged under ice as his eyes fell on the headline.

'Fishing boat lost at sea. Captain's family left without their father.'

The boat on the page was his father's tuna boat.

"No! No! It can't be! This has to be a dream. Quick, slap me! Wake me up!" Jake screamed, grabbing Gordon by the collar.

Gordon shoved Jake back, snarling at him like he had gone crazy.

"This is no dream, boy. Your incompetence has killed your father. Now your sisters are left with nothing. They blame you; they never want to see you again."

Jake sat sobbing in a ball in the lighthouse cabin, watching Gordon walk down the hill to his truck where Jake's sisters were waiting, clinging to each other, crying.

Jake woke with tears staining his face. His chest felt heavy and ached like his heart had been ripped out. He felt loss and guilt, regret tugging at his stomach—nausea set in. Jake scrambled to his feet and grabbed his cell. He dialed his father's number and sobbed harder when he heard his father's sleepy voice groan into the phone.

"Why are you calling at this time in the morning?"

Jake paused. He held his breath. "Sorry, Dad, go back to sleep," he said, trying to hide the catching in his voice.

"Everything okay, son?"

"It is now, Dad. Good night."

Each night, the nightmares threatened, and Jake found it harder to go to sleep. An anxiety Jake had never felt filled him; his appetite faded to nothing. No matter how much his stomach rumbled and ached, the thought of food made him feel sicker.

What if I don't wake up? Jake thought. *What if I wake up one day and it's not a dream, and people died because I couldn't do my job? Dad works at sea; I can't mess this up.*

Three days had passed since the nightmares had started. It felt difficult even to lay down. On the fourth night of his final week, Jake didn't know if it was sleep deprivation or a lucky turn, but he finally had a restful, dreamless sleep.

6
_____

JAKE WOKE FEELING WELL RESTED and famished. He hadn't eaten in days. The last food delivery of the week was due that morning. Jake couldn't wait. The thought of food made his mouth water. Hurrying to shower, dress, and turn off the light, Jake sat waiting.

He had slept peacefully, dreamlessly, and felt like a new man. Curious about what could have caused such violent nightmares, Jake pulled up his laptop. He had never suffered from nightmares before, not even as a kid when his cousins would try and scar him with ghost stories and pranks. Jake had always been logical, analytical, and level-headed.

Typing away at his laptop, he Googled for answers. He searched about what could cause nightmares, specifically night terrors, their meaning, and how to prevent them. Each article he found left Jake with more questions than answers. No one had a solid reason for nightmares or how to avoid them. Some articles put it down to stress and worry; Jake liked that answer. He had been worrying about doing the job right, making his father proud, and how he would help care for his sisters once he moved out. Another website put nightmares down to a lack or over-abundance of a mixture of certain minerals in the body. Jake had never been a fussy eater; he practically ate everything and anything put in front of him. Although since moving to the seaside town, he had eaten a lot of fish he had never tried before, some he had never even heard of.

Probably a toxin in some exotic fish, he thought; *maybe I should actually research my food before I eat it.* He remembered the chicken salad sandwich Kate had eaten. *Mmmm food!* He ordered takeout and again sat in wait. Too much time passed. *Where is this delivery?* he thought. *I'm starving.*

Jake curled up with his laptop and loaded up a movie on Netflix. It was a horror he had put on his top-watch list long ago. Despite his nightmarish sleep of late and against better judgment, he thought he should watch it.

Just as the movie was becoming too much for Jake, he was saved by a knock on the door. A delivery boy not much older than Jake stood in a bright blue and yellow tracksuit with a matching cap. Two large brown paper bags in his arms were packed full of food; the smells made Jake's stomach rumble.

"Delivery," smiled the boy, whose name tag said he was David.

"Thanks, man. Yo, come in. Those look heavy," Jake said, opening the door a little wider.

David looked inside and shook his head, taking a step away.

"Nah, man, I'm cool. How are you holding up?"

"I'm cool. What's not to love? Easy job, great pay, and I get to spend my days watching my shows and surfing," Jake lied, hoping his fake smile didn't betray how he was truly feeling.

"Braver than me, dog," David chuckled, kicking the ground at his feet.

"What is it with everyone and this place? I met some girls at the beach the other day, and when I said I worked here, they practically ran away!"

"Surely you know the stories. Everyone whose name is in that damn lottery knows the stories," David said, his face serious. He was upright and no longer kicking dirt.

"What is this lottery? The girls mentioned it too."

David's eyes grew wide, and his jaw fell open. Jake froze, waiting for David to answer.

"You...didn't volunteer, did you?" David asked.

"Yeah."

He looked at Jake with heartfelt sympathy, like he had lost someone; suddenly, it felt like they were at a wake. Then, shaking his head, David removed his cap and ran his hand through his thick dark curls.

"Hate to tell you this, bro, but this place is haunted — *cursed* or something."

"You don't believe that do you?" Jake laughed.

"Man, listen...."

David told Jake how the lottery was developed and how no one had volunteered for the role for many years. He told Jake about the stories his parents had told him when he was a child: about the lighthouse keeper who owned it before Gordon. He even told the stories from his grandparents. Jake stood there listening, frowning.

"So, if this place is so bad, why does it always have one permanent resident?" Jake smirked.

"It is passed down through the family. When Gordon retires, his son will take over. I heard one rumor that Gordon and his family are involved in witchcraft or something, and that's why they are cool to be here." David told Jake that two weeks out of the year, the lighthouse "needs fresh blood," as if the process was a ritual. He shrugged his shoulders after saying this.

Jake looked at David, waiting for the punch line, but none came. Finally, bursting out laughing, Jake swatted David on the shoulder.

"You're crazy!"

"Man, I'm serious. Ask anyone about the guy who came out a few years ago. A kid about our age...He survived the full two weeks but hasn't spoken a word since. He has night terrors; he hardly eats and jumps at his own shadow. Had a good future ahead of him, too, a talented football player, but now? Not the same kid. Then one girl whose name came up in the lottery jumped off the cliffs days after she came out. You couldn't pay me enough to stay in that place!"

Jake fell silent. He had stopped listening when David mentioned night terrors. Jake had started having nightmares, but he wouldn't admit it. Admitting it would be like admitting something sinister was going on. And if Jake could deny everything, then all the stories people told him were just that, stories.

"Well, I don't know what to tell you. I've been here almost two weeks, and it's been great. I've been surfing and chilling and slept like a baby apart from the odd cold night. So maybe this curse is broken," Jake laughed.

David smiled. "A curse can only break once. You're right; maybe this is it. I hope you are right, brother. I hope to see you on the other side. I got to go — got other deliveries to do. Take care," David said, offering his fist for Jake to bump.

Jake smiled back and watched how David practically sprinted back to his car and drove off in a cloud of dust, just as fast as Gordon had the day he left.

As Jake unpacked his food and tucked into a portion of freshly made eggs benedict, he wondered if David's stories had a truth to them. David wasn't the first to act funny regarding the lighthouse, and everyone he spoke to couldn't understand why he had volunteered. A part of him wanted to search for stories about the lighthouse online. But Jake knew if he permitted his mind to believe them, he would allow himself to be scared. If he read something he didn't like, he knew he would leave, and the rules were he had to stay the whole two weeks or he wouldn't be paid.

I've come this far, he thought. *A few nights of missed sleep is worth it. I'm almost done. I can do this.*

7

JAKE WOKE to hear a tapping at the door. Rubbing his eyes, Jake opened the door to find no one there. It was a crystal-clear night outside. The moon gave the night air a calming feel. Convinced he was hearing things, Jake headed back to bed. Gently drifting off, Jake heard another knocking, this time louder. The knocking grew with intensity, getting louder and more frequent with a sense of urgency. Finally, annoyed, Jake leaped out of bed and headed to the door.

As soon as his hand wrapped around the silver doorknob, the knocking stopped. Confused, Jake stood waiting. When nothing happened, he turned to go back to bed. Then, the door leading into the lighthouse started to thunder. Something, or someone, was banging heavily, trying to force its way into his room.

Jake ran to the cabin door, trying to escape, but it was locked, and the key was missing. Jake was trapped in his small room. There was no way out, and something was trying to get to him.

Jake rummaged through his delivery bags for his cutlery. Then, grabbing his knife, he clung to it tightly like his life depended on it. Curling up into a ball against the wall, Jake felt like the walls were closing around him as the door shook on its hinges. The knocking turned to clawing and howls. Both men's and women's voices howled in fear echoing through the small room. Jake closed his eyes tight, praying to make it out alive.

Jake leaped from bed, gasping for breath, covered in a cold sweat. He thought the nightmares had ended. Pacing the small room, he told himself repeatedly that it was all a figment of his imagination and that David had freaked him out. Then, feeling brave and needing to calm his chaotic mind, Jake took his flashlight and opened the door to the lighthouse. Waving the light around, he saw everything was normal—no evidence of monsters on the other side.

The next night, Jake had another nightmare. This time, he was changing the bulb when he heard men's and women's voices screaming. They screamed in terror and fear, crying out for help, for someone to save them. When Jake looked down the ladder, he saw a group of faceless strangers scrambling up the ladder, calling his name and begging for him to help them.

With only three days and two nights left before his time in the lighthouse was done and he could put the whole experience behind him, Jake tried to convince himself it was all in his head. But how could it all be in his head when every time he closed his eyes, he could see faceless people climbing up the lighthouse ladder towards him? How could it be in his head when everyone had warned him? Jake had always been a sound sleeper. But by the second to last night, he found every noise, no matter how small or obvious what it was, had him curled up under the covers like a frightened child.

"I can't do this," Jake said aloud.

Deciding not to sleep that night, Jake forced himself to stay awake and sleep through the day when he knew it was safe. Nothing ever happened during the day. Jake thought he had made the right choice when he slept through the day and had no dreams.

His cell phone rang one morning; It was the mayor.

"Good morning, Jake. Just to warn you, there is a big storm coming. Gordon had heard of the storm on the news and called ahead. He said the crank would need turning day and night when the storm hits. Also, the lighthouse is old, so it may not withstand the force of the coming wind; make sure you check everywhere and shore up the place with boards and nails if need be. Good luck."

Jake's heart sank. How was he going to stay up all day and night? Heading up to the top of the lighthouse, Jake saw that the sky above was black. Thick heavy clouds then rolled in, bringing claps of the loudest thunder Jake had ever heard. Lightning flashed across the sky so bright he was forced to shield his eyes. Waves crashed against the shore; the seas were furious. Jake hoped his father wasn't out on the tuna boat that day.

Suddenly, the alarm screeched through the lighthouse. Climbing down the ladder, Jake began to crank the lever.

"This is going to be a long day," Jake said.

Talking to himself had become a way for Jake to try and stay sane in the recent chaos of the seemingly innocent lighthouse.

The orange light flickered on and off. Jake had hoped the mayor was wrong and he could take a break. But as the wind crashed against the lighthouse, Jake knew there would be no rest for the wicked. Jake's shoulders ached from turning the lever, but finally, the light stayed on long enough for Jake to rest.

Not wanting to waste a second, Jake ran down and ate his fish supper as quickly as possible before the alarm sounded again. Then, running back to the lever, Jake began cranking once more. His body and mind felt like they might break. The stress of a sleepless twenty-four hours and the physical stress of the crank seemed almost overwhelming. Jake didn't know if the job was worth the money and perks. A slow drip of rain fell through the cracks in the roof and dripped on Jake as he cranked. When he finished cranking and felt the power satisfactory, he grabbed a few boards and some nails from a corner. A small ladder stood nearby. He got to work.

"Just one more day. Just one more day," Jake chanted.

8

THE STORM BEGAN to ease as day broke. The sun broke through a few gaps in the clouds. But the sky was still dark, and rain dripped through the roof's cracks. Satisfied that he wouldn't need to crank the lever again, Jake stretched. His shoulders strained. It hurt to stretch his muscles, but Jake knew he wouldn't sleep unless he did. His lower back hurt when he twisted his spine, and his knees clicked when he bent them. His stomach growled, and his mouth was dry. Over the last twenty-four hours, he had neglected himself, spending almost every second fixated on the crank to keep the lighthouse going.

Jake's eyes were red and dry from lack of sleep. And the roof hadn't offered much shelter from the pouring rain. His clothes were soaked through, his hair stuck to his head, and his soaked clothes made him shiver against the cold of the lighthouse. Sneaking down and out to the small back house for a hot shower, Jake freshened up and raided the fridge.

Jake ate until his stomach was full, wrapping himself tightly in his blanket and letting the warmth disrupt the chill in his bones. His mind still raced, thinking of the nightmares of previous nights. But no matter how much he forced himself to stay awake, his body fought harder. Then, slowly, the sound of the rain gently tapping on the window, the sea birds singing their song, and the waves gently lapping against the shore offered a soothing melody. Warm in his bed, listening to the bay sounds, his heavy eyes gently blinked closed until sleep finally claimed him.

Jake's mind drifted to the dreamland he was used to. As he slipped deeper and deeper into sleep, he dreamed of the promised house. He dreamed of working with his favorite movie stars and the look of pride on his father's face when the man was finally proud of him.

It felt like Jake had slept for a whole day when he finally woke up, but he didn't mind. It was the best night's sleep since he arrived at the lighthouse. His body felt fully rested, and his mind felt at ease. Keeping his eyes closed, he stretched and smiled, thinking of the life he was about to lead thanks to the job he had taken that no one else would.

"Finally, it's over," Jake whispered. He fell asleep.

A loud alarm forced Jake to open his eyes. It wasn't the lighthouse alarm. That alarm sounded like a fire alarm, loud and electric. It was almost metallic, a wailing thud like a hammer slamming against a bell. That's when Jake took note of his surroundings. The bed swayed as if in motion; he no longer saw the desk with his laptop or the window by the door. Alarmed, Jake sat bolt upright in a room with dark wood-paneled walls; a four-drawer dresser sat next to his bed, and the only light came from a small round window just above his bed.

Pulling himself up, Jake peered through the window. He was at sea. Panic setting in, Jake ran to the door, and his body grew cold. Outside his door was a long corridor full of other doors. People were panicking, running through the hall, and children were crying, clinging to their parents.

"What's going on?" asked an older lady to a man in a ship's uniform charging past.

"We are approaching port, but we can't find the lighthouse," cried the man.

"Wait? I'm on a ship?" Jake panicked.

Slamming his door shut, Jake sank against the door. Clutching his head in his hands, Jake began to sob in frustration.

"This is a dream. It's a dream. I'm going to wake up," Jake cried.

Slapping the side of his face, he cried harder, "Wake up! Wake up!"

Slapping himself harder, Jake stopped. He had never felt pain in a dream, but he felt that slap. He clawed at his arm and watched his skin turn red. It wasn't a dream. He was wide awake, wild-eyed, and terrified. How did he get there? Where was he? Jake ran to the window, searching through the darkness to see what he could see.

The waves crashed violently against the ship's side, and the moon hid behind the clouds offering no aid. It was too dark; Jake couldn't see a thing. Then, a long white flash of lightning cracked against the black canvas sky. It was hard to see, but for a second, Jake saw it. The rocks were five miles out from the lighthouse. The ship sailed in the storm heading straight for the bay. Straight towards the labyrinth of jagged rocks — straight into death.

Jake's mind flashed to the first nightmare he had. The bodies lay bent and contorted against the rocks. The water ran red, and a ship remained tangled in the bay. Was his nightmare actually a premonition? Had he borne witness to his own death? Not wanting to stick around and find out, Jake searched his mind for a solution.

"The ship needs to turn! I need to find the captain!" Jake said.

Jake knew if he could reach the captain, he could help. Even with the lighthouse not in sight, he knew the bay. He had studied it for the last two weeks. Running from his room, he charged down the corridors searching for anyone who looked like they worked on the ship.

JAKE HAD BEEN SO TAKEN BACK by waking up suddenly on a ship. Jake had been so fixated on finding a solution to his current problem that he hadn't stopped taking in his surroundings. A loud crack of thunder made the women on board erupt into a new chorus of screams, both plaintive and terrified. Another blinding light flashed through the ship's many windows lighting the cabins.

The flash had been the trigger. The trigger to make Jake stop and look around. He wasn't just on a passenger ship filled with people sailing to their watery graves. Instead, he appeared to have traveled back in time. The ship was like nothing he had ever seen before. The walls were a mix of dark and light wood paneling, the gloss on them scarred with age. The windows were round metal portholes, and the lights on the walls were all lit with candles, not lightbulbs. Some of the candles were guttering, and a few had gone out. Wind swept the corridors and created pockets of darkness. Jake walked more slowly through these spaces.

The floors were covered in a dark red floral carpet. But the fashion stood out to him the most. The women all wore floor-length corseted dresses and long-sleeved coats with frilly cuffs. Some looked like movie stars, while others looked like scullery maids. Some women were presented with hair pinned up and glittered with jewels and makeup, while others looked like they hadn't bathed in days. On the corridor wall leading to a small staircase, one sign said lower class, and another said first class.

The men were dressed the same: long fancy black wool suits, crisp white shirts. Some men wore monocles and had thick handlebar mustaches. They had top hats; hair gelled back so slickly it looked wet. Jake felt he had traveled back maybe one hundred years, if not further. At that moment, panic aside, Jake wished he had paid more attention in history class.

As he ran past a room that looked like a dining room, Jake caught a glimpse in the mirror that stopped him dead in his tracks. A larger gentleman with a thick European accent slammed into Jake's back. Scrambling to their feet, Jake looked the man dead in the eye as he was shoved backward.

"Watch where you are going, fool!" snapped the man.

"Sorry," Jake yelled after him. The man looked sideways with anger and lunged around a bend.

Jake turned and headed back through the crowd of panicked people, searching for safety. Pushing through the sea of people, Jake found the room with the mirror. His jaw dropped as he looked at his reflection. The person in the mirror wasn't himself.

Staring back at him was a tall man whose face appeared the same age as his father's. His cheekbones were high, and he had a long angular nose. A thick brown mustache and trim beard lined his jaw. He wore a brown plaid collared cape and a matching suit. Long black —like riding boots —traveled up to his knees. Jake removed the brown plaid flat cap from his head, revealing a slick, dark, brown haircut gelled to one side, a few whitish-gray hairs across its length. Who was this person looking back at him? He didn't recognize himself.

A harmony of shrieks erupted across the ship as it tilted to the side, threatening to subside. Jake was thrown across the cabin, smashing into a set of doors and shattering the glass panels. Jake pressed his hands to the floor, trying to stand up, and glass ripped through his skin, sinking deep into the muscles.

"Ouch!" Jake cried out, eyeing the blood over one hand. His vision caught a few drips falling to the floor.

Seeing this blood brought a thought of savage confusion to him: he definitely wasn't dreaming. Navigating the corridors, Jake charged, looking for the captain.

Jake might not know how he got there, who the man in the mirror was, or how to get home, but he knew he had to try and save these people. Men, women, and children were aboard the ship, traveling for reasons unknown to Jake. A new home? A holiday? Or for work? It didn't matter; they were innocent lives that needed saving. His new mission was clear.

Jake found a room where the ship's captain fought with the wheel at the bow. Sailors dressed in blue and white suits and wearing sailors' caps shone torches into the night, searching relentlessly for any signs of the lighthouse. Their boots weaved about the floor planks like many crows alighting.

"Captain! I can help!" Jake yelled, charging toward the man with a large white beard.

"I do not have time, sir," the captain roared over the sound of the waves.

"We need to turn. We are heading straight for the bay. This wooden ship won't stand a chance against the rocks in the bay. Everyone will die," Jake yelled, not recognizing his own voice.

"That is what I am trying to prevent," the captain replied.

Jake looked around the room and saw a table with a map that swayed with the ship. Grabbing the map, Jake examined it and waved it in front of the captain's face.

"Have you lost your mind?" yelled the captain.

"You need to listen to me! Turn the ship, and we might avoid the bay."

The captain grunted and grabbed a tall, strong-looking sailor who stood nearby.

"Johnson, man, the wheel."

The captain followed Jake to the table, where Jake slammed down the map. Then, Jake pointed out the best path to the shore with his finger.

"According to this map, our path is clear. We just need to navigate the storm," the captain shrugged.

"Trust me, captain, there are miles of jagged rocks straight ahead. It's a maze we will not make through. But, trust me, I know these waters," Jake insisted.

"Mr. Locks, while I know you mean well, I will need you to step back."

Mr. Locks? Jake froze, watching as the room around him fell silent to his ears. His mother's maiden name was Locks. His mind flashed with stories from his mother about how his great, great, great grandfather had traveled for a work trip and never returned. Had he been lost at sea? Was he looking at the world through his ancestors' eyes? Was he reliving his death as if it were his own? Would he ever escape this? He felt some unknown anger emerge, and he became more determined.

A loud smashing sound erupted from the side of the ship. The boat lumbered about the water like an injured monster. It shook and rocked as the captain struggled to turn the boat's course.

"We are sinking!" screamed the voices of the terrified passengers.

"Captain, listen to me. That was the first collision. If you do not change course now, we are all goners," Jake yelled. He shoved the captain aside, grabbing the wheel to pull it clockwise.

"Locks, man, are you mad? Arrest him!" screamed the angry captain.

Four sailors grabbed Jake, pulling him back from the room, but Jake fought harder. He had to do something.

"Captain...." Jake yelled.

"There is the lighthouse!" one of the sailors yelled.

Jake searched the horizon but could see no light.

"Rocks! We are going to crash!" screamed the crew.

They had found the lighthouse. But it was too late. The ship was too close. The captain tried to turn, but all he did was trap the ship further, leaving no way to escape. The captain's stubborn nature and reluctance to accept help had doomed them all. With each crash, the boat fell apart. The rocks and the storm shredded the fragile vessel apart. The ship split across and yawned open, wood beams exploding and splinters flying about. The passengers struggled away from this, and many on deck were tossed overboard, swept away by dark and hungry waves. People clawed past each other as the boat capsized. Those who didn't drown were smashed against the rocks. And the few not topside were entombed by the demolished doorways and caved-in halls underneath. More cracks of thunder boomed across the sky, and over the snapping and breaking of wood, people called out to each other in the darkness. Those with families called out names but were unanswered. The sounds of death became a slow conversation.

The winds calmed as the storm abated, and the rain slowed to a gentle trickle. The howls of the dying, the pleas for help, began to fade as light returned to the bay. Hope was a phantom here. Most realized help wasn't coming and became quiet before drowning. A few had struggled more and been taken underway before dawn. Jake blinked, trying to stay awake in the water, fighting to stay alive. Bobbing against a rock, he clung to it, his head aching, blood trickling into his vision. Finally, blinking light in the distance made Jake raise his head. The light from the lighthouse was the last thing he saw as the sun rose over the horizon. But it was too late.

10

THE FAMILIAR SOUNDS of the bustling town welcomed Gordon home. He smiled while driving in his pickup truck, thinking of how relaxing his two-week vacation had been. The townsfolk waved as he drove past, welcoming him back home. Just after sunrise, the store owners were opening up, preparing for the day ahead while the rest of the town slept peacefully.

Pulling up to the lighthouse, his home, Gordon stretched his legs back as the morning light framed the lighthouse in a beautiful orange glow. It was still early, and Gordon didn't want to risk waking the young lad who had been caring for his home in his absence.

Seabirds cawed overhead, and the breeze was warm and soft. Lighting his pipe, Gordon strolled down to the beach below. While others preferred the long miles of sand and waves, Gordon much preferred the bay beneath the lighthouse. It was always so secluded and empty; no one wanted to see jagged rocks and uneven terrain. But there was something about the chaos of the bay that soothed Gordon. There were patterns to it that he could enjoy.

The bay had history, a history the town seemed to have forgotten. But Gordon hadn't forgotten and never would. None of his family would because it was their responsibility to man the lighthouse — their burden and curse.

Directly under the lighthouse was a large wall depleted by the assault of the salty sea over the years, but a plaque almost as old as the town itself always seemed to survive. Hunting for the small spot on the wall, Gordon caught a glimmer of gold thanks to the sun's reflection. Wiping the metal clean with his hand and cleaning them off on his pants, Gordon looked up at the reason his family manned the lighthouse generation after generation. The plaque was a reminder of his family's past.

The plaque told the story of the many lives lost due to the lighthouse failure and how Gordon's family would be cursed to man the lighthouse until the end of their days. On the day of Gordon's return, it marked the one hundred and thirty-second anniversary of the passenger ship crash.

"I shall never forget," Gordon breathed, pressing his hand on the plaque. He muttered some names from the plaque: "Marin, Josephson, Locks, Kenton, Tillery...." Looking down to the ground with a blank expression, he thought to stop and recite the Lord's prayer, and instead walked away.

Gordon was approaching his last few years as the lighthouse keeper. Soon it would be his son's turn. And when that time came, he would tell his son about their family's past, failures, and the curse. Gordon looked at the curse with a partial fondness. He hoped to tell his son that all the rumors the townsfolk spoke of were true and how it was best to avoid the lighthouse during those two weeks in summer. There was a pride to these hopes; he wanted his son to understand the risk in taking his throne and always felt himself a protector of the town. He would tell the boy of the time when the ghosts of the dead came to land to get revenge for their untimely deaths.

This was the general idea. But Gordon held some more hurtful considerations to himself. This haunted past was not a past for the sake of those lost. For some, it was a child far away and struggling in the darkness of unknown water, unable to answer their parents; it was a person taken apart by a plank of wood; it was the minute before entirely drowning. It would not suffice to have only general ideas about what happened in honoring those lost. But his son could wait to be told this.

Gordon felt terrible year after year, leaving an unexpected soul to deal with the curse. But if he didn't, no one would be there to man the lighthouse, and history would repeat itself — there would be another crash upon the rocks, another mass death if the light were not maintained. Gordon had given up years ago trying to figure out what the dead wanted or how to break the curse. He even had a séance conducted at the lighthouse, to no avail.

He just prayed that one of his children would before it became his granddaughter's burden to bear. She would be the first female to man the lighthouse, and Gordon didn't want that life for her. So, Gordon lived for his two-week vacation. Manning the lighthouse was a lonely task, and most townsfolk avoided him because of the mystery surrounding his home.

He cared more about his legacy than this rejection and felt these circumstances were almost honorable. Still, he regretted that such profound loss had manifested in this way. The curse was an unmoored vestige of the town, a stain that should be openly acknowledged and regretted. Most chose to cast it off; they were led by fear and superstition, not acceptance or understanding. Nobody wanted to help fix the problem; nobody cared but to sneer that it was a problem, that it simply existed — like cancer. There were no easy answers here.

Gordon strolled back up the beach, watching the morning light wake up the town. Youngsters ran to the beach to surf. Locals walked their dogs, and the town roared to life. Checking his watch, Gordon thought it was time to wake Jake.

Gordon knocked on the door gently, patiently waiting, but Jake didn't answer. So, Gordon knocked again a little harder.

"Jake? Wakey wakey. Let me in," Gordon chirped.

When Jake still didn't answer, Gordon traveled back down to the bay, entering a small cave beneath the lighthouse. Traveling through the tunnels past the scattered remains of broken ships and the skeletal remains of the victims of the sea, Gordon found the door to the cellar. It hadn't been opened in years, but with a good hard shove, he managed to open it. Climbing in, Gordon ventured inside.

Gordon searched the top of the lighthouse, turning off the light for the day. He climbed the ladder to the crank, but Jake wasn't there. Finally, he checked his cabin. The cabin was empty, Jake's possessions littered the house, and uneaten food sat in the fridge. The front door was locked, and its key lay on the bedside table. This sight would have alarmed others, but not Gordon.

Shrugging, Gordon tucked into the food Jake had left behind and resumed his post. The lighthouse creaked loudly as Gordon settled back in.

"I'm home, old girl; I'm home."

The End.

SWITCHED

1

MORGAN AND SOPHIE sat in the tree house Sophie's father had built her years ago. They huddled under the big blanket they had made from their parent's old band t-shirts many summers past. Though too old to play here much anymore, the girls had grown up together in this tree house. During water fights, they'd spent endless days hiding from Sophie's brother and bombarding him from above. Countless nights had passed as they'd slept over in the branches, telling each other ghost stories before running inside, scared when they heard rustling in the trees. The treehouse had been their sanctuary, safe space, and home to all their secrets. The girls clung to each other, not wanting to be pulled apart.

"It's crazy to think someone else is going to be using this tree house. It's ours; it doesn't feel right," Sophie cried.

Morgan pulled her friend closer, holding her tight while trying her best not to cry. She needed to be strong for her friend, despite her own breaking heart.

"They can take the tree house," she whispered, "but no one can take our memories."

Sophie's mom called up from the grass beneath them. "Sophie, you will have to come down at some point; you need to finish packing!"

"I don't want to move," Sophie cried harder into her best friend's shoulder.

Morgan rubbed Sophie's back, straining to hear as the hushed conversation between Sophie's parents floated up toward them.

"Are you going to tell them?" Sophie's dad whispered.

"No, I can't. It will kill them; this is hard enough," Sophie's mom replied.

Morgan's stomach twisted; something was wrong. More bad news? But she was already losing her best friend. How could things get any worse? A vague dread came to her, a loss for something unknown; she stopped crying.

Sophie sniffed, stood, and reluctantly started climbing down the ladder. "What are you two whispering about?"

"I'm sorry, sweetie, but I have some bad news," Sophie's mom stuttered. "The new owners had asked if we can remove the tree house before they arrive next week."

"The tree house? You can't!" Sophie shook with rage, sudden and clear, almost missing the blanket Morgan tossed down behind her. "Isn't it bad enough that I'm being *ripped away* from my best friend!?"

"It's not like we can take it with us, sweetie." She meant the tree. It was a passing fondness to Sophie now, already disappearing. There was a fog around it in her mind.

Morgan looked to Sophie's dad, who not so subtly hid his toolbox behind his back. It was time to leave. With the tree house gone, there would be no going back. This departure felt like the death of something — of memory.

"Come on, Sophie, I'll help you pack," Morgan offered, taking her friend's hand and leading her inside.

The girls boxed away Sophie's bedroom in silence, pretending not to hear the sound of wood breaking and crashing to the ground outside the window. Sophie began sobbing, deeply now. She was unmoving, stuck like a doll. Tears fell after a few moments. Morgan rushed over to pull the curtains shut, but not before catching a glimpse of the last remains of the tree house. The wooden beams burst apart against the force of Sophie's dad's hammer, collapsing and crashing to the ground until the branches were bare. The scars in the dark wood were now the only sign that the treehouse, or Sophie and Morgan, had been there.

Darting across the room, Morgan hooked her phone to her still unpacked Bluetooth speaker, queuing up her favorite pick-me-up playlist. "There, no more crying. I don't know how much more I can take," she said, forcing a smile. "We still have a few more days together. Let's make them the best."

With that, Morgan grabbed Sophie's hand, dancing around the room like a crazy person until her friend burst out laughing.

The rest of the week passed in a blur of packing. They found new memories, spending those last days in the park and the mall, taking as many pictures as possible, sleeping over at Morgan's as much as possible, and staying up late watching movies. They mostly tried to avoid thinking about the ever-decreasing countdown to the day Sophie would leave.

Finally, the dreaded hour came. Sophie and Morgan sat on Sophie's doorstep, watching as the moving men packed their furniture and Sophie's parents loaded the car.

Sophie wiped her cheek with the back of her hand. "I can't believe it's finally happening. It's gone too fast."

"I know. I wish you could stay too. But mom said if it's okay with your mom, you can always come to visit," Morgan offered.

Sophie sniffed, pulling herself to her feet. "I have a present for you. Wait here." She ran into her house and returned moments later with a large package wrapped in colorful tissue paper and topped with ribbon.

"Sophie, you didn't have to do that," Morgan said. "I feel so bad I didn't get you anything."

"It's nothing special, but I want you to have it."

Morgan nodded and tore open the paper. Inside was a blanket decorated with the logo of their favorite band. They had made it together, using a steam iron to apply the art onto the cotton fabric.

"I want you to have it. You have been the best friend a girl could ask for. But you are more than a friend. You are like a sister to me," Sophie laughed, elbowing Morgan's side. "Plus, if you have the blanket, it gives me more reason to come back."

Morgan flung her arms around Sophie's neck, hugging her tight.

"I love it. I love you. You are my sister too," Morgan cried.

"No! Don't you start crying. You are the strong one. If you cry, I'm going to start crying again."

Sophie's parents called her away. Morgan stood beside her mother, waving her best friend off. The moving truck engine roared, pulling slowly from the driveway, the departure marking the end of an era.

Morgan's vision blurred. There was no chance of Sophie and her parents returning.

2

————

MORGAN LOOKED out of the window of her bedroom. Her mother was walking across the street to the new neighbor's house, carrying a plastic container of her famous mac and cheese — a welcome gift for them. It was something her mother did whenever someone new moved in. Morgan's mother always said community was important and made a point of getting to know all their neighbors.

Morgan saw a young couple appear in the doorway of her friend's former home: a tall blonde woman emerged, her hair tied into a tight ponytail. She had brown highlights. She spoke to her mother, seemed very friendly, and had a smile so big and bright Morgan could see it shine from her room, glinting light like on a glass surface. The young woman introduced her husband to Morgan's mother. Tired of watching them chat away, Morgan tucked herself back into bed and continued to flick through her photo albums, remembering a happier time with her old friend. The loss of touch with Sophie felt almost controversial.

"Honey, you need to break out of the slump," Morgan's mother said over dinner.

Morgan pushed her food around her plate, not interested in

eating much. She had lost her appetite since Sophie left. Grunting her reply, Morgan didn't look up from her plate.

"I'll make you a deal. You eat your dinner, go upstairs, and do your homework before school restarts next week. And I will let you use my laptop to Skype with Sophie, and I'll even let you stay up late. How does that sound?"

"Really?" Morgan asked excitedly.

"If it puts a smile back on your face, then yes."

Morgan smiled and finally felt good enough to finish a meal. Tucking into her mother's mac and cheese and finishing it off with a hot fudge sundae, Morgan hugged her mother and ran up to start her homework. Morgan hadn't told her mother that she hadn't done much of her homework over the summer break, so she had a lot to catch up on. But she knew if she hunkered down, she could get it done.

Math was first — algebra. Morgan hated algebra. Sophie was always better at it. Setting it aside, she thought she could ask Sophie for help when she called later. She did what she could and put it aside. Swiftly polishing off her English assignment, Morgan moved on to history. A woman on a mission, she poured all her focus into her work until something caught her interest.

Filled with a sudden feeling of being watched, Morgan felt a chill take her. Pulling the band blanket around her shoulders, Sophie glanced out her window. The house opposite – her new neighbors – was enveloped in darkness. The cars were gone from the front of the garage. She assumed they had gone out for dinner, but a light was on in the third floor's top window.

Stepping closer to her window, Morgan looked out. A boy about her age was standing in the window, staring back at her. Morgan blushed, brushing stray hair behind her ears. She thought he was cute and tall, with dark hair and features that reminded her of a pop star. Morgan watched as the unblinking boy stared back at her, his face expressionless.

When they moved in that morning, Morgan couldn't remember seeing the new family with a boy, but she had quickly slipped away to her room. Perhaps he was home doing his homework, bracing for school as well. Morgan and the boy looked at each other for a while. His eyes did not move away from hers. Then, feeling a little awkward, Morgan smiled and waved. The boy didn't move. She waved again, and he remained still. Mortified, embarrassed, and red-faced, Morgan acted as if her mother had called her, mumbling the words "Be there in a sec," giving herself impetus to close the drapes quickly.

"Hey honey, how are you getting along?" her mother asked, knocking on her door and popping her head inside the frame.

"All done," Morgan smiled, happy for the distraction. She took a deep breath.

"Very good. Here, have fun. Do you want hot cocoa?" Her mother handed over her laptop.

"Sure, sounds lovely. Extra marshmallows, please."

"As always," her mother chuckled.

Morgan couldn't wait to talk with her friend and find out if Sophie was missing her as much as she was missing Sophie. Waiting for the screen to load, Morgan fidgeted in anticipation. Then, finally, the screen roared to life, and Sophie's face smiled back.

"Oh my God, Morgan, I've missed you so much," Sophie roared, her face beaming with her bright smile.

"I've missed you too. How's California?"

Sophie told Morgan about the cute boys on her street, how her parents have been trying to encourage her to make friends, and about her new school. Sophie always liked the heat, so she was loving the California sun. From her glowing skin, it loved her too.

"So, have the new family moved in yet?" Sophie asked.

"Yeah, and I had the strangest experience with their son."

"Ooooh, do tell," Sophie chirped, clapping her hands.

"Nothing like that. I saw him watching me through the window. He just stood there staring. I waved, and he didn't even blink. I pretended mom shouted at me so I could close the drapes. It was so embarrassing," Morgan cringed.

Sophie laughed hard until her friend laughed with her.

"The important thing is...is he cute?" Sophie winked.

"Oh, super cute. He looks like a pop star, you know, the type of guy to break your heart," Morgan mocked.

"Oh my god, I love him already. Did he look like one of the guys from our band?" Morgan did not reply. "He was probably just as upset about moving as I was. Introduce yourself when you meet him at school. You never know; next time we talk, you might be writing his name all over your notebook," Sophie laughed.

"Sophie, no," Morgan chided, smiling.

"I miss you, girl."

"I miss you too," Morgan smiled again, feeling somewhat obligated to talk to her mother when she walked in with her hot cocoa.

3

MORGAN WASN'T ready to go back to school without her best friend beside her. But her mother reminded her that she had other friends too.

"Martin is still in school, and I know how close you and Sophie are with him. You will have a great day. The first day back at school is always a drag. I remember a time when...."

"Please, Mom, I don't need another one of your once-upon-a-times from the olden days," Morgan teased.

Her mother's mouth fell open in mock shock and horror. She clutched her hand to her chest, looking visibly pained as if suddenly wounded by an unknown force.

"Oh, the day hast come when my offspring mocks my age. How will I *ever* move on?"

Morgan and her mother burst out laughing at this absurdness. They hugged, and lunches were packed; Morgan headed off down the street to catch the school bus. As she walked past Sophie's old house, she looked up at the third-floor window. Sophie may have left, but a new kid across the street meant new possibilities for friendship.

Morgan thought back to the night before, remembering how the boy looked. His hair was medium-brown, not curly; his eyes were blue and sharp. She wondered if he was a little older than her and if she would see him in school.

If he isn't in any of my classes, I might just pop over after school to introduce myself, Morgan thought.

ONCE SCHOOL BEGAN, all the students were summoned to the assembly hall. As the school did every start of the year and term, it was the school's customary welcome back speech. As the head teacher talked to the crowd about her plans for the new school year, projects for the school's clubs, and the sports team's successes, Morgan scanned the faces of her fellow students.

Like Morgan, not many other kids were listening. Some sat with their faces glued to their phones, others whispered amongst themselves, and a few even sat with their heads bowed, having a quick morning nap. There were rows and rows of students, all in grade order. The new kids usually sat along the side of the assembly hall to observe before being assigned to their new classes, but Morgan couldn't see the boy from across the street in the row of eight new students.

Well, he could be in a higher grade, and there are a lot of faces here, Morgan thought.

With no luck finding the face in the crowd, Morgan sat with her eyes faced forward. Nodding and smiling along but, like her fellow classmates, not truly paying any attention to the head teacher.

"Now, class, I'd like you all to offer a warm welcome to your new classmates," chirped Mrs. Lydia, Morgan's teacher.

Morgan's head shot up from her notepad, where she had been doodling while the rest of her class arrived. Excited that she could be meeting her new neighbor, Morgan stretched her neck to see over some of her taller classmates. Three figures entered the room, but Morgan still struggled to see them.

"Class, please welcome Jordon from New Jersey, Lauren from Ohio, and Christian all the way from England...We were expecting another student, but it looks like they may have gotten lost," Mrs. Lydia smiled, clapping her hands and encouraging the class to follow suit.

Morgan stood from her seat to catch a glimpse of the new boy. But the boy in front of her was pale with freckles that took over his face and thick red curly hair. He was not the handsome young man from across the third-floor window.

"Sorry, I got lost. Is this Mrs. Lydia's class?" asked a raspy Texas accent.

Morgan's head shot to the door, expecting and hoping he was whom she was looking for, but no. Yet again, Morgan found disappointment.

Morgan carried on her day, as usual, getting her head stuck into new assignments and engaging in the school's debate club. Yet, no matter how she tried to busy herself, her mind wandered to the boy in the window. Every hallway she turned around, she would see a face in the crowd or a silhouette, only to be left looking the fool when she approached and realized it wasn't him either. She knew she was searching for him and felt haunted by this motivation; an infatuation was creeping through her, severing her attention to common tasks. Math class especially became a daze. She forgot briefly how to divide, blushing privately at the loss.

Even at lunch, as Morgan listened to her friends chat about how they spent their summer break, Morgan scanned every face that walked into the cafeteria and every face that lined up to be served. She felt fraught with this process but could not stop herself.

"Looking for someone?" Loretta asked, snapping her fingers in front of Morgan's face.

"What? Oh, no, just in a world of my own," Morgan smiled back.

"You have been like this all day. You have been picking at your lunch for the last twenty minutes. Sophie moving really messed you up, didn't it?" Michael asked.

"Yeah, I miss Sophie," Morgan admitted.

On the bus ride home, Morgan admitted defeat. *I bet he goes to one of those fancy private schools uptown*, Morgan thought. *His parents looked like they had money from the furniture I saw them moving with.*

"HEY SWEETIE, HOW WAS SCHOOL?" her mother asked when Morgan tossed her school bag on the kitchen counter.

"Okay, I guess. Nothing exciting happened. How was work?"

"Same old, but I had a lovely chat with our new neighbors. Natalia, her name is, really liked my mac and cheese and brought over a wicker muffin basket as thanks."

Morgan was suddenly alert, listening to her mother talk about Natalia and her husband Lucas like she had made two new best friends. Drinks had been arranged for the weekend, and the new family was organizing a barbecue for a few weeks from now, when they were settled in, to get to know everyone.

"Wow, they sound so cool." Then, Morgan began, "What about their kids?"

"They don't have any. Natalia had several nieces and nephews and said she likes to share the fun times with them and give them back to their parents at the end of the day. I thought it an odd comment, but I laughed anyway."

"So, no kids?" Morgan asked again.

"No, just man and wife," she smiled cautiously.

4

CURIOUS AND CONFUSED, Morgan was distracted for the rest of the evening. Finally, when her mother kept asking if she was okay, Morgan lied and said she had some tricky new assignments in school she was trying to figure out.

Eventually, curiosity got the better of her. Making excuses to go to bed early, Morgan headed to her room. Peeking through the drapes, her heart skipped a beat. In the third-floor window, standing as if he hadn't moved since the last time, was the boy.

Morgan opened the drapes, and the boy didn't move, staring unblinkingly back at her with the same blank expression. Morgan waved, this time not getting scared, and waited for him to wave back. He didn't. Thinking the boy was a bit odd, Morgan decided to finish her homework at her desk. Trying to act like she wasn't bothered, she kept checking to see if the boy was still there. Peeking out the corner of her eye, the boy didn't move. He continued to stand there watching Morgan at work. It was a liminal sensation, his eyes on her, sitting at her desk as if he were in a corner somewhere. She was not scared because she was alone in many ways. She only knew he was there by sometimes peeking at her window, thinking it was somewhat strange for him to just stare into her room, though it felt comfortable enough, given the distance. Her door was locked, and her window closed. The event was like passing a rainy sewer drain clogged with some moving but unrecognizable debris. Her eyes bent again toward the window as she was finishing her essay.

Finally, Morgan grew tired. Closing her drapes, she headed to her en suite to wash her hair and prepare for bed. Fully relaxed, she sank into bed, where her mind was still on the boy in the window. Who was he? Why did his parents deny he exists? And why did he keep staring? ...Does he exist? Morgan dreamed that she was screaming for him to talk or even blink. But like a statue, he stood watching.

Perplexed and a little disturbed by the dream, the first thing Morgan did on waking was check to see if the boy was still there. When she saw he wasn't, she assumed he was either still sleeping or had headed out to whatever school he attended.

Sitting with her mother for breakfast, Morgan brought up the new neighbors. She wanted to know everything her mother knew about them. Natalia was a wedding planner and spent most of her day traveling, talking to suppliers and venues, and spending most of her weekends at different weddings. Lucas was a photographer who specialized in marketing smartphone photo editing apps. He had worked on some pretty impressive campaigns, and Morgan realized she used one of the apps. He sometimes helped photograph the weddings Natalia planned. They were a good pair, her mother said.

The new couple had recently married and bought their first house together. But being such career-oriented people, neither wanted children. Morgan was amazed by the amount of information her mother knew from just a few short conversations over an exchange of dishes. But Morgan's mother was the type of woman who could stop a stranger on the street and discover their life story.

"Anyway, enough blabbering, you better get ready for school," her mother said, shooing her away as she cleared the table.

Morgan showered, brushed her teeth and hair, and put on a very minimal amount of makeup. Then, packing her bag, she found herself drawn to the window. The boy still hadn't returned, but she watched as Lucas emerged from the house. With thick, messy blonde hair and a matching beard, he wore torn dark jeans and a plain white T-shirt. His camera was strapped over his shoulder, and he had a travel mug of coffee in his hand. Morgan watched as he got into his BMW and drove off with music blaring through the car windows.

"Morgan, you are going to be late. Hurry up!" her mother yelled up the stairs.

Hurried not to miss the school bus, Morgan quickly hugged her mother and grabbed her lunch before rushing out the door. As she left, she watched Natalia in a bright fuchsia pantsuit and killer high heels rush to her car; holding her phone under her arm and struggling with a pile of folders, she hurried into her car and drove off at speed.

As Morgan waited for her school bus, she kept a close eye on the house, waiting for the boy to leave, but no one else left the house. She practiced watching the window from the corner of her eye for a few moments. The strain of this gave her a slight headache. She sighed and got on the bus.

5

UNABLE TO STOP THINKING about the new couple and the mysterious boy in the window, Morgan decided it was time to talk to someone about it. Was it an obsession? Did she need help? With Sophie unavailable for a video call, Morgan turned to the only other person she trusted. Her second best friend, Michael.

"Hey M, how are you? I missed you yesterday, but it looks like we have Biology together today," Michael said, giving Morgan a soft tap on the shoulder.

"Yeah, I think we have English and History together too," Morgan smiled.

The bell rang, indicating it was time for the students to head to their next class. Pushing through the overcrowded, loud hallways, Morgan listened to Michael talk about his fishing trip with his father and grandfather and the monster truck rally he went to with his older brother Simon.

"How was your break? How are you holding up since Sophie left? I'm so sad I didn't get a chance to say goodbye," Michael said, dodging one of the older students charging through the hall.

"I miss her. The new neighbors have moved in now, too," she replied.

"Wow, what are they like?" Michael asked.

They entered their biology class with Mr. Jones, who told the students to sit down quietly, *please,* and get ready for the class to begin, cutting Michael and Morgan's conversation short. Morgan and Michael didn't get another chance to continue speaking until lunchtime. Michael noticed the same thing their other friends had sitting at the lunch table. Morgan was picking at her lunch and was very distracted.

"So, you were telling me about your new neighbors. What are they like?"

"Oh, right. Strange really —" Morgan answered.

"How so?"

Morgan told Michael that when Natalia and Lucas moved in, she hadn't noticed their son with them. She explained their jobs and everything her mother had told her from the conversation with Natalia.

"That seems pretty normal. Is something off?" Michael inquired.

"Well, the night they moved in, I opened my drapes and saw a boy about our age, maybe a little older, in the third-floor window. He was standing and staring, kind of like a statue. He didn't blink or move, I waved at him, but he didn't react."

"He was probably shy."

"That's not the strangest part. I didn't see him in school yesterday, and when I got home, my mom said they don't have kids. But he was at the window again last night, watching me."

Michael chewed on his lunch for a moment, deep in thought. "Maybe he is home-schooled."

"But why would they say they don't have kids?" Morgan asked.

"Well, he sounds a little odd, staring, not moving or reacting. Maybe he is special, and his parents are embarrassed? So, they might keep him hidden because he is dangerous —" he caught himself: "No, maybe he's autistic or something." He paused to drink from a pint of milk. "Some people are like that...."

Michael's choice of words shocked Morgan. If the boy was dangerous, was she safe living across the street? Her mind raced with possibilities. She had hoped that talking with Michael might ease her mind. Michael was usually a very logical person, he gave great advice and always made sense, but now all Morgan felt was anxious and more curious than ever. The more she thought about it, the more questions popped into her mind.

A thought occurred to her. Loading up her phone, she searched for local amber alerts for a missing boy who matched his description. Unfortunately, no amber alert came close, and the search yielded only five results. Most of them were girls, and the boys were much younger. She expanded her search for regional and national alerts, but the results were far too many to search through. She would be there for hours.

"What are you doing?" Michael asked, snatching her phone and scanning through the results.

"What if they kidnapped him?"

"Come on, Morgan, why would they leave him alone if they kidnapped him? He could escape while they are out of the house," Michael argued. "Besides, he's more likely to be autistic than violent...right?" He seemed very unsure.

"What if he's *locked* in that room?" she barked.

"Good point, but why wouldn't he try and get you to help him if he were trapped?"

Morgan couldn't argue with that point. She knew if she had been kidnapped, she would do everything she could to alert someone who saw her. Why hadn't he done more than stand and stare? She pondered, moving to a new question.

"What if they are holding him against his will? You know, like holding him prisoner. He could be their son, but they might be scared he will run away. Like if he had tried to run away before," Morgan offered.

"Same answer; why isn't he doing something about it? Does he realize he *should* do something about it?" Michael asked, the lack of good answers feeling like a dismissal of the subject.

Morgan snatched back her phone and searched for articles about Lucas and Natalia, but without knowing their last name, she couldn't narrow down the search. So, she explored a little harder and found Natalia's wedding planning website. The 'About Me' page described Natalia, her marriage to Lucas, and how they met in high school. Pictures detailing their life together showed holidays, their wedding day, and them growing together over the years. In many photos, the borders were vacant, mostly white or black spaces with centralized images. Why wasn't a Christmas tree seen alongside one of them unwrapping a gift? She could understand the wedding photos showing mostly the married couple, but even the bouquet toss showed women packed together in the middle, with no chairs or others nearby, like a herd. A subsequent photo displayed the woman who had caught the red pastel bouquet, again centralized, standing between Lucas and Natalia. The woman looked into the camera blankly, and the bride and groom seemed distracted by something off-camera. This display did not seem ludicrous; she shrugged all of this off. No images showed children, and there was no mention of kids either.

Another search led her to Lucas's photography page. His pictures were incredible, momentarily distracting Morgan from her purpose on the site in the first place. Scanning his About page, she found a similar description and photographs to Natalia's page. Nothing of interest.

Several minutes had passed. "Why are you so fixated on this guy? Is he hot?" Michael teased.

"I won't lie. He is cute, like super-cute. But it's more than that. Something just feels off about the whole thing. I need to find out about him and know he is safe."

"Are you sure this isn't just your way of projecting? You were always like a big sister to Sophie. Perhaps you are missing her more than you think, and this is your emotions manifesting in a new project," Michael shrugged.

Morgan gave his comment a bit of thought. Sophie was only a year younger than Morgan, and they had known each other since they were old enough to walk. Morgan had fought off bullies and helped Sophie learn to skate and ride a bike without realizing she had taken on a protector and big sister role in their friendship. But she didn't look at the boy in the window like that. Even if she was naturally protective by nature, the churning in her gut and strain in her chest told her something more profound and sinister was at play.

"What's wrong with that? Say you have a point. Is there anything wrong with me wanting to help someone?" she asked.

"Not at all. In fact, I think it's great. But don't get yourself all twisted and bent out of shape. Does he seem harmed? Unfed? Unsafe? What is it that makes you feel like he needs saving, or that there is something to worry about?" Michael asked.

Morgan thought hard about the boy. She hadn't really paid that much attention. She couldn't remember if he seemed scared or unsafe. He had a healthy face, not overly thin. Apart from his looks, all that stuck in her mind was his strange, unmoving behavior. His staring. *Gosh*, was he handsome.

"You may have a point," Morgan sighed, admitting defeat.

"Look, I can tell you care. I've always admired that about you. It's why we are such good friends. You have such a big heart. Keep an eye out. If you see anything that stands out or if he makes an attempt to ask for help, talk to your mom. Until then, don't worry so much."

6

KEEPING MICHAEL'S words in mind, Morgan decided to monitor the house from her window for the rest of the week. Pulling out a spare notebook, she began to make a log. First, she noted when Natalia and Lucas left and came home. Next, she noted when she saw anyone leaving or entering the house and what times the boy appeared in the window.

The first night she watched him from afar, acting like she wasn't watching and continuing her homework and other tasks around her room. Every time she did something new, she noted down the time, the task, and if the boy moved, which he never seemed to do.

The second night, she made large signs to hang in her window. The first said hello, but still, the boy didn't respond. The next sign asked if he spoke English, but there was no reaction. Frustration started to pool in her stomach. She was trying to check on his wellbeing, and not once had he responded.

Boy in the window didn't respond to my signs. Can he read? Is he blind? Why doesn't he move? He acts like a statue, staring right through me. What is going on in Sophie's old house? Am I going mad? What if he is a statue? Very realistic if so. Could it be a deterrent against robbers when Natalia and Lucas are out of the house?

Morgan wrote more and more. The third night she tried again with more signs.

How are you?

Can you write back?

Are you safe?

My name is Morgan.

Growing tired of getting no response and from lack of sleep, Morgan closed the drapes and headed to bed.

On the fourth day, as with every morning following since she began the observations, she noted the moment she woke, the weather when she checked if the boy was there, and what she was doing. Every morning he was gone. Morgan checked her window multiple times before leaving for school, but it appeared the boy was never present past sunrise.

"How is the stakeout going?" Michael asked at lunch on the fifth day.

"Nothing new to report. Look," Morgan slid her notepad across the table.

Michael scanned page after page, his eyes growing wide. Finally, closing the book, he slid it back and looked at Morgan with concern.

"Morgan, this is crazy. You are becoming obsessed — this is too much."

"What would you do?" Morgan asked.

"Ha! Probably the same," Michael admitted.

Pulling the notebook back, Michael looked over her notes. Nodding and skimming page after page.

"Why haven't you been taking pictures? Any good detective would also collect photo evidence,"

"That would be going too far. I'm pretty sure that would be breaking some kind of law."

Morgan laughed, even as she considered it a good idea.

"True."

BY THE END of the week, Morgan decided to simply watch. With her homework done and no plans for the weekend, she snuck down and collected some snacks and a thermos of hot cocoa. She wrapped herself in the band blanket and sat at her window watching the statue of the boy. He was always in the same clothes, the same position, and the same window. In the early morning hours, Morgan grew excited, finally noticing that the boy blinked once. Scribbling notes of this, and with a new sudden burst of energy, Morgan sat up, alert.

> *Boy in the window blinked. He is definitely not a statue. I was stupid to think that. It is now three forty-five, and he hasn't moved once. He is wearing the same clothes he has worn since the first night. He doesn't seem to be distressed or hurt; not even his clothes are dirty. His complexion is clear, and he seems well-fed, with average weight. He is showing no signs of stress or fear. All seems relatively normal. So why are they hiding him?*

Getting bored and her eyes heavy, Morgan pulled her laptop to her knee and loaded up Google. She typed in the boy's description and searched, but her description wasn't specific enough and only brought up generic images. Trying another approach, she searched for articles about a boy who had run away and been found. Again, nothing matched the boy in the window. Finally, she tried for articles about a dangerous boy to see if she could find a reason his parents might be keeping him hidden, but again came up empty. Morgan's eyes grew too heavy as the sun rose, and she drifted to sleep.

Waking, she rushed to her window to find the boy was gone.

Damn it! she thought. I wanted to track when he left the window. I will have to try again tomorrow.

Morgan knew she couldn't stay awake another night on the run, not with the weekend drawing to a close and school approaching. So instead, she set the alarm to wake her up an hour before sunrise. Waking up at five in the morning, Morgan was pleased to see the boy was there. She didn't want to miss him leaving the window. She hoped if she could watch him leave the window, she might get some answers. What else was in the room? Did his parents come to collect him? But before she could get the answers she craved, she drifted back to sleep, waking to find the boy was gone.

Oh, come on, this is crazy. Is he playing games with me? Morgan thought.

Frustrated, she gave up, rolled over, and went back to sleep.

7

"MORGAN, get up. It's almost noon. What's wrong with you, sleeping so late?" Morgan's mother woke her Sunday morning.

"What? Noon? Wow, sorry, Mom," Morgan yawned, stretching her muscles and climbing out of bed.

"Everything all right?"

"Sure," Morgan smiled.

"I have a few errands to run today before I finish my project for work. Fancy coming along for the drive? I might even stop off for a treat on the way home."

"Sure, sounds fun," Morgan smiled happily for the distraction.

Morgan waited for her mother to leave her room before rechecking the window. The boy was definitely gone. After Morgan got ready, she headed downstairs and had a healthy lunch with her mother before they headed out. While her mother took a call from her boss, Morgan stepped closer to the house across the street, again fixated on the third-floor window. The room in question had once been Sophie's bedroom. She wondered what had been done to it now. Was it the boy's bedroom? Was it his prison? Or had they simply left it empty to place him there every day — as if the room were a storage container?

"Morgan!" her mother yelled, snapping Morgan back to reality.

"Sorry," Morgan chirped, skipping back to the car.

"What's with you lately? You are always distracted and fixated on that house."

"It's nothing. I just miss Sophie and our memories in that house," Morgan lied, deflecting the topic.

"I know you do, dear, but it will get easier, I promise."

Morgan and her mother spent the day shopping for groceries, picking out new curtains for the living room, and a few other tasks her mom needed to take care of. After their day off shopping, Morgan and her mother went to the nail salon and finished their day with a coffee at Starbucks.

"Thanks for today, Mom, it was fun," Morgan smiled.

"Anytime, my love."

When they got home, Morgan helped her mother unpack the groceries and began her chores. They laughed, joked, and danced along to the radio, enjoying each other's company. It was a welcome distraction for Morgan.

"Where is your gym uniform? I'm about to do the laundry," her mother asked.

"It's in my bag in the kitchen," Morgan replied, wiping down the coffee table. The reflection in it was a dark mirror.

A few minutes later, Morgan's mother appeared in the doorway holding Morgan's notepad. Her face was grave with concern.

"Morgan? What is this? Are you stalking our neighbors? And what's this about a boy being kidnapped?"

Morgan turned, and her jaw fell open, her eyes fixed on the notepad.

"Mom, you're reading my stuff?" Morgan yelled, running across the room and snatching the pad from her mother's hands.

"It fell out of your bag, and I was concerned. Morgan, what's going on?"

Morgan stood silently, not knowing if she should tell her mother, who stood blocking the doorway, her arms folded, waiting. The expression on her face, which Morgan knew well, said, 'I'm not moving until you tell me the truth.'

Sighing, Morgan took her mother's hand and led her to the couch. She explained what happened the day the new family moved in and her concerns about the boy in the window. Morgan explained her notes page by page and her fears that Natalia and Lucas were not who they said they were.

"Morgan, you can't be serious?"

"I am, Mom. I'm really worried. If they are keeping someone in their house, who knows how much danger we are in."

"Look, I know Sophie leaving has been hard...."

"Mom! I'm not making this up!" Morgan snapped.

Morgan glanced at her watch; it was almost dinner time. She knew how crazy her theory might sound to anyone who hadn't seen the boy. Even her best friend Michael had a hard time believing her. The only way she could convince her mother she wasn't crazy was to show her. Taking her mother's hand, she pulled her to her feet.

"Morgan!"

"Come, Mom. I'll show you, then you will *have* to believe me."

Reluctantly, her mother followed Morgan to the room. Morgan pulled her drapes wide and pointed to Sophie's old bedroom.

"See, look!"

Her mother stepped closer and stared, examining every window in the house.

"You are being silly. You need to stop watching ghost videos on YouTube before bed," her mother laughed.

"What?" Morgan looked, and to her surprise, the window was empty.

The boy was nowhere to be seen, yet she had seen him there every night for the last week at this same time. So why was he gone when she needed him to be there? A pit in her stomach approached her throat; she gulped a breath of air, nervous now.

"Mom, I promise he was there. But, wait, he will show up."

"Morgan, I have dinner to prepare and a project to finish for my deadline tomorrow. Really, darling, you are getting far too old for these childish games!"

"It's not a game. I'm telling the truth," Morgan insisted.

"You know I wasn't going to say anything, but I got a call from your teacher on Friday. They have said you have been distracted all week. If you put this much effort into your schoolwork, maybe I wouldn't be getting phone calls from school voicing their concerns on the *first week back*," Morgan's mother said, clearly annoyed. "I'll call you when dinner is ready."

Morgan sat on her bed feeling deflated. It had been a long time since her mother had snapped at her like that. She feared she had let her mother down, especially because of school. Had she dreamt the entire thing? Was she simply missing her best friend? Again, was she going mad?

Morgan sat and watched the window, but the boy never showed. Finally, deciding she was under too much stress, Morgan headed downstairs to watch television while her mother cooked dinner.

Morgan and her mother didn't speak through dinner, Morgan was too embarrassed to talk, and her mother was tapping away at her laptop between bites. Finally, with the meal finished, Morgan let her mother continue her project while she cleaned up and loaded the dishes into the dishwasher.

"I'm going to bed," Morgan said, kissing her mother on the cheek.

"What? It's only six thirty," her mother said in surprise.

"I'm tired, and I have school tomorrow," Morgan said.

"Morgan. I didn't mean to snap at you earlier. I'm just concerned. This behavior isn't like you. I'm your mother and just want to make sure you are all right."

"I know, Mom. Good night," Morgan smiled.

Morgan headed to her bedroom, prepared her school bag, and laid out her clothes for the following day. Then, firing a quick text to Michael and one to Sophie, Morgan climbed into bed. When she reached over to close the drapes, she saw it. Gasping, she froze. The boy was back. She wasn't going crazy and hadn't imagined it.

"I'm going to find out what's happening in that house. Just watch me," Morgan said, closing the drapes and slowly drifting off to sleep. She dreamed of the space between their two windows and how windy it was. The wind kept increasing. There were whispers to it. And suddenly, many dull eyes hung there in the dark, just outside her curtain. They were reaching for her.

8

———————

"To be honest, Morgan, I didn't expect your mother to believe you. So, don't be mad, but I thought you were crazy at first, too," Michael said once Morgan explained the events of the night before.

"Thanks, pal," Morgan laughed.

"I know that laugh; you're planning something, aren't you?"

Morgan nodded. Pulling her notepad from her bag, she presented the page she had prepared on the bus ride to school. Michael looked over the notes, the times, and the questions Morgan had noted down.

"So what? You're planning to break in?" Michael joked.

"No, of course not. I'm going to watch the house, find out everything I can about Natalia and Luca's routine, and I'm going to go over and introduce myself. I will be the perfect neighbor and get them to invite me in. Then I'm going to look around. I will find out what is happening in that house, and then *you* and my *mother* can stop thinking I'm crazy." She de-emphasized this last word, her lips pursing upon it.

"Well, you are doing a great job so far," Michael teased.

For the rest of the week, Morgan watched the house as closely as she could without her mother getting suspicious. Then, finally, when Natalia came for drinks, Morgan tried to sit and join the conversation, but her mother told her to leave them be. They were having 'adult conversation,' she said. But Morgan couldn't be deterred so easily and hid outside the conservatory door, listening and noting everything about Natalia's life and day-to-day routine.

"So, did you and Natalia have a good night?" Morgan asked over breakfast the next day.

"We did. I think I may have made a new friend," her mother replied.

"That's nice. She seems pretty cool. It seems they live pretty separate lives. They both come and go at such odd times, always rushing. It must be lonely for her. She could use a friend like you," Morgan said.

"Not really. Yes, they have their own jobs, but Natalia said when they are home, they spend a lot of time together." Morgan could not confirm this; she changed the subject. "Do you have a lot in common? Like, what does she like to do in her spare time?"

Morgan's mother eyed her suspiciously but chose to answer her questions anyway.

"She likes to read, she likes movies, and she sews. That beautiful suit she wore the other day she made herself. So talented. I wish I could do that. She can crochet, too."

"Did she talk about Lucas? I feel like I know a lot about her but not much about him. He seems pretty cool. He said hi to me a few mornings when I was on my way to catch the school bus."

"What's with all the questions? I feel like I'm being interrogated," her mother mocked.

Morgan fell quiet. She hadn't prepared herself for being questioned. What excuse could she give? It wasn't like she could tell her mother what she was planning.

"I've just been so sad since Sophie left, and you made me see I wasn't dealing with it very well last week. You are such a good neighbor; getting to know everyone, I'd like the chance to do the same," Morgan answered, thinking fast.

"Well, that's lovely, dear. I have always told you the importance of being a good neighbor," her mother smiled proudly.

"I was thinking about baking some cookies and taking them over to introduce myself. Do you think that would be okay?"

"I think that is a wonderful idea. How about when you get home from school today, we bake them together, and then you can take them over tomorrow after school?"

"I would like that," Morgan answered.

"I STILL THINK YOU ARE CRAZY," Michael laughed. He was again drinking milk. The color of the pint container was different, but Morgan couldn't pinpoint how.

"Then come with me tomorrow. My mom won't mind," she said.

"Ha! No thanks, I don't want any part of this charade. Sorry kid, but you're on your own with this one." Her mom would call her a *kid* sometimes too. She brushed this off.

The rest of the school day seemed to drag. Morgan found she couldn't keep her eyes off the clock, but clock watching always did make time slow down. Counting down the hours, minutes, and seconds until she could get home, Morgan fidgeted with her pens, bounced her leg, and raced to the school bus at the end of the day.

Keeping up the facade that she was the best neighbor, Morgan baked the cookies with her mother when she got home and insisted on taking them over when they were fresh from the oven.

"Good heavens, no, it's dark outside, and it's late. Go to bed. You can go when you get home from school tomorrow," her mother argued.

That night, Morgan fell asleep watching the boy. His eyes were unmoving, two rocks in a cave. She slept a little better that night, knowing she was one step closer to finally getting the answers that had haunted her for almost two weeks.

THE TIME WAS FINALLY upon her. Arriving home from school, Morgan ran inside excitedly and grabbed the decorative basket of cookies her mother had left on the kitchen counter. From what Morgan had observed, Natalia and Lucas's routine was hard to pin down. Sometimes they didn't come home until late evening. Other times, they were home before Morgan got back from school. Morgan hoped that someone was home that day.

Morgan's hands shook, and her heart raced with every step closer she was to the front door. Something about the house seemed different. To Morgan, the house had a darker, more ominous feeling about it. The gables shook with wind, and every edge of the roof gave to thick looming clouds. She saw the boy's window and looked away immediately.

Standing in front of the door, Morgan took several deep, slow breaths before raising a shaking hand and gently knocking on the door. A few moments passed with no answer. Morgan knocked again, this time a little louder, but no one answered.

Morgan walked around to the side of the house where the car was usually parked. She didn't know why she hadn't checked there first. No cars, no answer. No one was home.

So close, yet so far from finally having answers, Morgan felt a sinking feeling in her stomach. She didn't want to wait much longer. She had come so far, too far, to give up now. Her hand reached into her hair to curl a few strands, then dropped to her side. She pondered fear for a moment.

"I'm not leaving until I have answers," Morgan said to the house. Wind swept over her, and the structure groaned in response. Its windows rattled slightly.

She didn't know or care how, but she was getting inside.

9

MORGAN SAT the cookie basket on the doorstep and checked to make sure no one was on the street watching her. Once the coast was clear, Morgan checked all the usual places for a spare key. Unfortunately, Sophie's parents had many fun locations to hide the key. Under the door mat, the plant pot, on top of the door frame, and in the flower beds. Morgan checked everywhere, but the new neighbors had either hidden the key somewhere new or neglected to leave one at all. In hindsight, it was probably for the best, considering Morgan planned on letting herself in.

Then, a thought occurred to her. Getting in was one thing, but what if the new couple had an alarm system? The police would be at the house in minutes, and all the neighbors would surely run out and catch her. So, she had to think smart. She knew the alarm system on her house had been installed, so she checked for lines around the house and peeked in through every window she could. Thankfully, the new owners hadn't had an alarm installed yet, making Morgan more determined than before to get in.

Morgan ran around the house, checking all the windows and the back door, scanning her surroundings once more. The house was locked and secure, but Morgan wasn't giving up without a fight. Pulling a bobby pin from her hair, she tried jimmying the lock to the back door, but all she did was bend the pin and grow more frustrated.

I wonder, Morgan thought. The moment was laid out before her.

Morgan remembered that when Sophie lived in the house across the street, she had hidden a key to the lock for the basement. At the back of the house by the porch were two large wooden doors that led to the cellar below the house. Morgan was pleased to see that Sophie's family had left on the old chain and padlock.

I guess they couldn't find a key for the lock. Luckily, I know where it is, Morgan chirped to herself.

Heading over to the tree, Morgan searched amongst the rocks at the base of the tree. In the middle was a small plastic rock with a false bottom. Inside was the key to the padlock. Sophie had hidden the key to help her sneak in and out of the house when she was grounded. Morgan never could figure out how Sophie had gotten away with it for as long as she did.

Checking her watch, Morgan knew she needed to be fast. Natalia or Lucas could be home at any time. So, turning the key in the lock, she yanked off the chains and snuck inside, carefully closing the door behind her.

The cellar was just as dark as she remembered it, the light switch was at the top of the stairs to the kitchen, and another was by the clothes dryer at the base of the stairs. Careful not to trip and fall, Morgan went into the cellar, into complete darkness. The wind was breathing heavily outside. When she reached the bottom of the stairs, she brought up an internal map of the basement in her mind. She smacked her hip on the clothes dryer two steps to the left. Reaching up, she pulled on the cord, and the cellar lit up.

Everything looked different. The clothes dryer and washer were exactly where Sophie and her parents had theirs, and the boiler was still just as creaky and scary against the far wall. The old shelving unit where Sophie's dad once kept his tools was gone, replaced by a gray back-zipped tent. Curious, Sophie pulled the tent open and peeked inside. Lucas had set up a small dark room to develop his prints. Careful not to let in too much light, Morgan snuck back out and made her way through the maze of unpacked boxes to the stairs leading up to the kitchen.

She entered the kitchen and saw everything was the same except the fancy new espresso machine on the counter by the fridge and the black and silver blinds over the windows. The silver of the blinds had a dull shine, with the black seeming like lines of void across the space of the window frames.

Moving into the dining room, everything was ultra-hip and modern. Blacks and chromes with silver velvet ceiling-to-floor curtains were held back with twisted white rope. How *Goth*, she thought. She had a vague idea of the subject. Michael had claimed he was goth once but wore normal clothing.

Morgan searched the first floor for any signs of the boy from the window. The living room above the fireplace had a vast canvas painting of Lucas and Natalia from their wedding day. It was gorgeous. All the other pictures around the house were the same; Lucas and Natalia but no child, all with a centralized focus, staring at the camera, standing and sitting. The only thing in the living room that could have belonged to a kid about Morgan's age was a gaming console, but Morgan deduced that it could also have belonged to Lucas; he had the look of a gamer, after all: somewhat geeky, wore glasses and was always stylish, an artist.

Heading upstairs, Morgan checked the master bedroom and the two guest bedrooms. One room had been converted into an office; by the heaps of wedding materials, it was apparent the office belonged to Natalia. The other guest room had been converted into a sewing room, with a mannequin draped in electric-blue silk and a partial cocktail dress pinned on its front.

Morgan knew the third floor consisted of two rooms. The room at the back of the house had a restricted view, thanks to the big tree out the back, and the bedroom at the front was Sophie's old room — the room Morgan needed to get into. As Morgan strolled up the stairs, her heart raced, and her mouth ran dry. She could be meeting the boy from the window in a matter of minutes. She was a bit scared but excited, her hands clenching slightly.

What will I say? What if he is dangerous? And how can I get us both out of here? Morgan thought as she came face to face with the large wooden door.

10

MORGAN TOOK hold of the giant golden door handle, but she was too nervous about opening the door. A sudden feeling of unease took her. A feeling told her to run and never look back, to throw open a hallway window and climb out if needed.

I can't give up now. I've come too far. Just open the door, Morgan argued with herself.

Turning, Morgan decided that as she had searched every other room in the house, she should at least check the back bedroom. Morgan admired the one and only guest room, dressed in whites and blush pinks with roses decorating the bedspread and the silver mirror on the dresser. She recalled the image of the woman with the bouquet in the wedding photo: similar colors.

With nowhere else to go, Morgan knew it was now or never. She had to see what was inside Sophie's old room quickly. The new owners would surely be home any minute. Walking across the landing to the door, Morgan took a deep breath and finally opened the door.

To her surprise, the room was empty, aside from a few empty moving boxes. Looking around, Morgan sighed and let her shoulders sag. How could this be? She had spent over two weeks watching this boy. How could not be here? No one had left the house since she entered it; where did he go? Were Michael and her mother right? Had she made everything up in her head to cope with missing Sophie?

Well, I guess it's all over, she thought.

Walking over to the window, Sophie examined it. A very faint handprint was still present on the glass. Resting her hand against it, she realized her hand fit the imprint perfectly. As her hand connected with the cold glass, the door slammed shut behind her, making Morgan jump and gasp.

Sophie did say that door had a mind of its own; Morgan laughed, trying to calm her racing heartbeat. The hinge must be off.

Staring out the window, Morgan looked at the street below. Even when she was over at Sophie's, she had never taken in the view from across the street. First, she could see the Robinson's three doors down and their new white rose bush. Next, she could see the Greens' house, with their twin's toys still littering the front lawn, and even the home next to hers owned by the Montana's, pristine as always. Then, as her gaze drifted over to her place, she saw her mom's car up the drive; she must have just gotten home from work!

I better get going before Mom realizes I'm not home, Morgan thought.

Morgan's eye drifted to her bedroom window, and she froze. The air around her felt like it was freezing, and her pulse raced. The boy from the window was sitting in her room, bent over her desk, seemingly doing homework.

"What the hell?" Morgan yelled.

Morgan panicked as she watched her mom enter the room with a cup of cocoa. She watched her mom place the cup on the desk and hug the boy around the shoulder.

"Mom!" Morgan yelled, tears brimming her eyes, causing them to sting and burn. She elbowed them away.

What was this!? she thought. How could her mom hug the boy? Didn't she realize he wasn't her daughter Morgan? Then the boy looked up at her mother, and the pair exchanged a smile and words. Morgan's ears began to ring. She felt underwater. The wind outside became much less audible.

Clutching to the windowsill to steady herself, Morgan forced herself to breathe. Her legs were jelly as she watched her mother exit that room.

"Mom! Mom! It's not me! Mom!" Morgan yelled. She quickly became hoarse from this; her ears popped, and the wind returned in full force.

As if he heard her or sensed he was being watched, the boy tentatively raised his head, scanning the room. Then, slowly he turned his head, and his eyes locked with Morgan.

"Hey! Get out of my room! Who are you?" Morgan yelled, hammering her fist on the window.

The boy walked over to the window and shyly waved at her. Morgan froze as if watching herself do the same thing only weeks before. Too scared to do anything else and confused, she saw the clouds in the periphery of the window sweep away. All Morgan could do was stare back at him. The boy's face changed; he looked startled and embarrassed. Then, in a rush, he closed the drapes, and Morgan watched the room go dark in the thin crack left open.

"No!" Morgan yelled, hammering her fists hard against the glass. "Come back!" Morgan screamed. The glass cracked, and the wind came in; she felt colder, numb. But the sounds were louder than normal. The wind was screeching now; even indoors, it sounded dangerous. Then it suddenly died down, and fog set in.

Running to the door, Morgan tried to open it, but it was locked. She tried and tried at the knob and shoved the frame with her shoulder, but the door wouldn't budge. Finally, slamming her fists against the wood until the door shook, Morgan screamed for help. Kicking her feet into the door as hard as she could, hoping to break down the door; nothing she did worked. The door was too thick; solid oak.

Tears streamed down her face as fear rushed through her, making her feel sick. Bile rose in her throat, burning her and leaving an acid taste on her tongue. A care engine hummed outside the house. Running to the window, Morgan saw Natalia pull up, closely followed by Lucas. Morgan watched as they got out of their cars, greeting each other with a hug and a kiss.

"Hey! Up here! Help, I'm locked in! Help!" Morgan screamed.

No matter how hard she slammed her fist against the glass or how loud she screamed, the couple didn't seem to hear her. Instead, she could hear their muffled voices from downstairs. Kicking and punching the door, jumping up and down on the floor, Morgan kept calling for help, but none came. Her foot was injured from the kicking.

Limping back against the door, Morgan scrunched herself into a ball on the floor. Then, pulling her knees tight to her chest, she began to sob. She couldn't understand why no one could hear her. She couldn't understand how her mother had not realized the child she had hugged wasn't her daughter. Who was this boy, and what had he done to her?

Suddenly, a high-pitched screech sent a cold shiver down Morgan's spine and filled the room. Looking up, Morgan's breath came thick and fast. The windowpane where her handprint had once been became fogged up. The window became like a chalkboard as lines began forming across its glass. Something invisible was writing on it, the sound deafening as words etched above the cracks she had made in the glass.

Morgan's eyes grew wide, and her body temperature dropped as she stared at the words on the glass. She couldn't remove her eyes. Game rules appeared and immediately faded from view.

```
Current High Score: 100 years.
```

"What the hell does that mean?" Morgan screamed, hoping something or someone would answer. She remembered a saying her mom always told her: be careful what you wish for. At that moment, Morgan knew why. Dread filled her chest, and hopelessness swamped her thoughts as more words appeared on the windowpane.

```
New Player. Ready to begin?
```

The End

HAUNTED

1

IT HAD BEEN a tough year at Riverside Junior High. To help raise the students' spirits and give them something to look forward to, the school announced a Halloween celebration. It was Mrs. Stuart, the art teacher, who had the idea. And after much persuasion, the other teachers got on board.

A letter was sent to the parents requesting any help they could offer, and it didn't take long before the school was inundated with parents willing to volunteer: baked goods, decorations, organization of the event, costumes — everything the school might need help with.

"Guys, have you seen this? The school is hosting a Halloween haunted house this year," Alex cheered, joining the other kids at the lunch table.

"Really? How lame," Blake complained.

"I don't know. It sounds cool. They will decorate the entire school like a haunted house. Each classroom will have a different scare attraction, and then there will be a dance with a buffet," Drew chirped, tugging the flyer from Alex's hand.

Blake shrugged, reluctantly offering a smile of defeat. "I guess it could be fun."

"Look, it's a costume party!" Avery cheered.

The group of friends loved a good costume party. Being some of the most competitive kids in school, they always strived to have the best and most creative costumes, be it in school fairs or costume parades.

"Okay, now I'm interested. What's everyone going as?" Blake chimed in.

Discussions began. They tossed the obvious choices about — killer clown, zombie, vampire, witch. Then the conversation turned to movie characters and pioneers from history. Each student had a fun and vibrant personality. They were forever considering the good of humankind and how they could change and save the world. They wanted their costumes to make a statement and be seen. They wanted their ideas displayed to convince people they were good and to learn more about their subjects.

"I wouldn't do anything political," their teacher said, aiming a pointed look at Avery. "I hear there will be a prize for the best costumes. Categories are fitting the general theme, which is obviously Halloween. Best Scary Costume, Most Unrecognizable Student, and Most Imaginative," continued Mr. Flanigan. They continued shooting costume ideas.

Mr. Flanigan was everyone's favorite teacher. He was what they all considered "cool." He was always "in" with the latest social media trends, movies, and music and gave the students a heads-up on things he felt they would benefit from — in this case, the Costume Parade.

"Okay," Alex broke in. "Then we better get our thinking caps on. How cool would it be if we all made our costumes connected and we all won a prize?" Alex asked.

"Well, there are four categories and five of you," Mr. Flanigan chimed in, stuffing a red M&M in his mouth.

The students looked at him, confused, counting their group before turning back to him.

"Sir, there are four of us," Avery chuckled.

"Nope, a new student just moved to town. A bit of an odd character, but I think they will be a great fit for this group. You guys have always been so welcoming in the past," Mr. Flanigan smiled.

"Sure, sir. When do they start?" Blake inquired.

"Already has; I'll inform them right away. I knew I could count on you all."

Mr. Flanigan moved from table to table, checking on his students while eating his lunch. After laughing about their favorite teacher and how they thought he was "cool," it was hilarious how much effort he put into being accepted by the students; the conversation moved back to costume planning.

The haunted house was all the students were talking about in the cafeteria. Speculation spread about which teacher would offer the scariest room and which teachers' rooms they would be avoiding. The Halloween celebration had swiftly turned into the event of the year and clearly had the desired effect of lifting everyone's spirits.

"Let's face it. Mrs. Luna isn't the most imaginative. So, I don't think her room will be much fun," laughed Avery.

Mrs. Luna was the home economics teacher, and some of her recipes for what she considered "fun" classes were always questionable. She once asked the students to make a recipe she found in a book she bought from a thrift store. She thought the recipe was a perfect mix of modern trends and history, new and old. The chosen dish dated back to 1947 and was called Avocado Ice Cream. To everyone's surprise, it was actually palatable. That wasn't the case for the Poor Man's Casserole they tried, however.

"I think Mr. Smith's room will be the best. He pulls pranks on his class every Halloween, and we all know he loves horror movies," Alex said excitedly. "On April Fools' Day, he pranks the teachers! He's always down for a laugh."

Drew chuckled. "I don't know. I think this might be too scary for me. You remember the story he told the class last year about the haunted asylum? I had nightmares for weeks about the straitjackets," Drew said and shook as though trying to shake off the memory. "I think I'll avoid his room. He takes scaring to a level I'm not cool with."

"Oh, come on, don't be like that," Blake teased, smiling and making pointy feline ears.

"I'd rather be a scaredy cat than have weeks without sleep," chimed in a voice behind them.

The group turned to see Mr. Flanigan smiling with the new student and member of their group at his side.

"This is the new student I was telling you 'bout," Mr. Flanigan smiled — "Charlie."

"Hi Charlie, come sit with us. We're talking about the Halloween haunted house next week. It should be fun. Are you into costumes?" Blake asked hurriedly.

"Am I? I go to Comic Con in full cosplay every year. I got a bunch of ribbons for my costumes," Charlie beamed, joining the group at the table.

"Then welcome to the club," Drew said, clapping Charlie around the back. "What's cosplay?" someone muttered. Charlie caught this and explained the costumes previously worn to the event.

Mr. Flanigan was right. Charlie fit into the group perfectly. Conversation flowed easily, and the group quickly gave Charlie the rundown about the school, their favorite teachers especially, and which students to avoid.

"Wow, you guys are fab. I've never had a welcome like this before," Charlie said, beaming with gratitude and appreciation.

"Do you move a lot?" asked Alex.

"I'm an army brat. But this is our last move. They have officially discharged my dad," Charlie answered.

"Welcome to Riverside High," beamed Drew.

2

HALLOWEEN COULDN'T COME QUICKLY ENOUGH. The week leading up to Halloween seemed to drag in anticipation. All week, the teachers dropped hints as to what their room would be like and which teachers they thought offered the least scary room. But one thing was for sure. True to form, Mr. Smith's music room was set to be the most frightening. He even had his students play some Halloween songs with their instruments in anticipation of the coming event.

Finally, the big day arrived. While the teachers and parents set up the school, the students were having an outdoor cross-country event organized by the gym department. The first clue that anything was going on in there showed up while they were eating lunch in the stands. It was a huge banner that read "HAUNTING BEGINS AT SUNDOWN." It was apparent that sundown would come earlier than usual when all the windows were blacked out. In reality, students would change into their costumes after lunch and head to the gym, which would be decorated last while the students toured the haunted classrooms.

Alex was the first to arrive at the gym. Waiting for the rest of the group to arrive, Alex watched the other students trickle in. The mix of costumes was incredible. The effort the students had put in was astounding: there were grungy pirates with wooden teeth; were-wolves hairiest at the nape of their necks and ears; movie stars young and old, many in sunglasses; Grammy-winning pop stars in rosy makeup; blood-soaked Walker zombies; various ghouls slopped in drooping fake skin; devils and angels — one wielding a cardboard broadsword painted with flames — and even a mermaid or two made their way into the school — one carrying a fishbowl filled with blue plastic beads and fake fish, another with a tail for legs.

"Alex?" came Drew's voice.

"Drew? Wow, you look incredible!" Alex chimed.

"Your costume is pretty cool, too. Break into your sister's theater makeup?" Drew laughed. Drew's face was covered in black whisker-like streaks and wore a short crop of dye-black hair. Drew laughed, clearly impressed.

"Who else was I to come as, Frankenstein?" Alex chuckled.

"I was going to go as a sorcerer but thought it was too generic," Drew said.

"A dragon trainer is a pretty impressive choice. I've seen a lot of witches and wizards passing by. No dragon trainers yet. Nice armor," Alex nodded.

"It moves too, watch."

A giant, animated green dragon puppet was wrapped around the shoulder of the armor and curled down around the breastplate. The controls for the puppet hid nicely in the neck, allowing for move-ment, and realistic dragon growls came with the press of a button.

"So cool," Alex awed.

"That's not even the best part," Drew rushed on.

Pressing another button from the inside of the puppet's head, a gust of air blew from the puppet's mouth, shooting out a wave of red, orange, and yellow ribbons to simulate the fire of dragon breath.

"Someone definitely wants to win a prize tonight," Blake's voice chimed in as the sea of students parted to let this Black Panther pass.

"Who doesn't want to win this, eh?" Drew grinned.

"What do you think of my costume?" Blake asked.

Blake gave a spin to show off the entirety of the costume, which had taken days to make. Lights lined the detailing of the superhero suit, and with a flick of a button, the Black Panther mask closed over the entire face with glowing purple eyes.

"Wow, someone raided dad's toolshed," Drew laughed.

"When else will I get the chance to be a superhero? My dad's an engineer, like Iron Man," Blake laughed, lifting their arms into a T-pose and flexing their biceps.

Avery was next to arrive in an extravagant and expensive-looking vampire costume fit for Broadway. The black and red velvet cape lined with gold trim glistened against the overhead lights. Vampire fangs perfectly fitted their mouth, very naturally, and the red contacts offered a piercing glare.

"I hate to disappoint you, Avery, but you are not the only vampire here tonight," Alex said, pointing to a coven entering the gym. They strutted in like a dance troupe on America's Got Talent.

Most of the other costumes were not as imaginative as Avery's; their makeup was basic white face paint, dark eyeliner, and fake blood dripping from the lips.

"I am not just a vampire. I am the Lord of the Vampires, Count Vlad Dracula. Let's see if any of their costumes can beat mine!" Avery spoke in the thickest Transylvanian accent they could muster, making the group laugh in wonder. The *oos* and *ahhs* were very pronounced.

"Wow, guys, you look amazing!" Charlie cheered, arriving last.

"Cool skeleton costume," Avery said.

They wore a skin-tight black body suit decorated with a glow-in-the-dark skeleton. The detailing was incredible, far more life-like than anything the group had seen before. Charlie pressed a button, and, in the chest cavity, a realistic human heart glowed and pulsed red. A slow thumping heartbeat emitted from the phone in the suit pocket.

"This is awesome, and the face paint is spot on," Blake awed.

"Thanks. My cousin is a professional makeup artist. We just had a mad dash session in his car. It usually takes hours to do, but we got creative. It might not hold as long as it usually does," Charlie explained.

"I can see why you've won ribbons at Comic-Con," Alex admired.

"Okay, we all look fantastic. Can we go now?" Drew said, jumping up and down excitedly.

As if on cue, the school principal made an announcement which was soon followed by a soundtrack pumping through the school's speaker system. The "Monster Mash" began playing. Whatever the song, the group was excited. The haunted house was expected to be great, and great meant scary. There were high expectations.

Red cloth draped down from the ceiling, effectively giving the harsh hallway lights a ghoulish red tint. In some corridors, the lights were off; replaced with flickered spots aimed at bloody handprints along the walls and ominous messages like 'RUN,' 'LEAVE,' and 'PRO-CEED AT YOUR OWN PERIL.'

A group of girls dressed as zombie cheerleaders ran screaming from Mr. Smith's room, one of them in tears. Their blood-red pom-poms shook down the hall and around a corner.

"Told you Mr. Smith was committed. Let's try his class first," Avery said, charging ahead of the group.

The group entered the maze of rickety wooden shelves that created a small labyrinth in the room. Each shelf had jars filled with the oddest things – small knobby growths, eyeballs, teeth, and twisted mold. Light glowed through the eyes of carved pumpkins, showing the way. Eyes of pumpkins flickered from the candles lit within their heads.

In one section, the ceiling was covered with hanging heads of various shapes and sizes. They weren't the plastic skulls you get from the dollar store. No, they were made of burlap and straw, like scare-crow heads. The severed heads wore shocked expressions, made more gruesome by their button-sown eyes. A hand clutched at their hair which was tied to the ceiling. The other heads wore bloated expressions, and Mr. Smith had added tiny hands clutching the rope around their necks.

As they continued through the maze, the students found creepy pictures of clowns smiling at them. And a fully formed human body made of papier mâché lay across a table, soaked in red corn syrup and purple bruise makeup. Ambient music played around the room; it sounded like the floorboards creaked with each step like someone was following them through the maze. The sound of footsteps and scuffling feet approached and withdrew. The music speakers were positioned, so the students often heard them behind their backs.

"This isn't so bad," Drew said. They spotted a tiny speaker behind one of the larger heads roped against a school desk.

As if waiting for a cue, thunder erupted in the room with a flash of light, making the group scream and jump. Finally, making it to the center of the room, the kids looked upon Mr. Smith: He lay face-up, chained to a table, his clothes blood-soaked and looking like the Big Bad of scarecrows. All his clothes were cut from coarse burlap and sewn together with thick black veins of thread; many seams were frayed and left open intentionally. From these holes oozed chunks of blood as if pumping from open wounds beneath the suit. A janitor was dressed as a clown and standing next to him, looming over him. The group did not recognize the janitor as being from their school; he either was a complete stranger, or his makeup and broad manic smile were too visceral to allow examination. The clown had fangs, and a blood-soaked axe was gripped in his right hand. With a swing of the axe, the clown appeared to chop Mr. Smith's entire body in half. The chunks of blood exploded from holes in the burlap, and his legs had been separated from his torso. But the teacher shot up from the table, his torso suddenly intact, a giant cleft across it; he let out a blood-curdling scream and spit fake blood across the floor. His arms lurched at them like an ogre grasping for a human meal.

"You're next!" growled the clown, turning and pointing the axe directly at them.

"Rise, my minion! Get your next meal!" ordered the clown. His smile quickly became a wide-eyed frown, his lips a gruesome and insane gesture.

Mr. Smith had been committed to his performance. The legs flailing on the table while the clown brought his axe down — even when obviously not his own — this offered the perfect distraction and realism for when Mr. Smith's torso turned towards the students and acted like it was chasing them.

"He isn't really going to chase us," Blake complained.

Speaking too soon, a group of actor friends of the teacher broke through the bookcases and shelves. They were living nightmares: a fury of blood and fangs and razor talons, brandishing ornate daggers and sickles, a tall scythe standing at the center of the swarm. They groaned and growled in approach, grabbing at the students and making them struggle to escape the maze of the room.

"That was...something," Charlie panted as they ran up the corridor to escape.

"Mr. Smith never disappoints," Alex laughed, feeling uneasy, goosebumps forming.

The rest of the rooms were not as impressive as the music teacher's. While some offered a little scare, others were just plain boring. However, it didn't take long for the group of friends to grow frustrated and annoyed.

"I didn't go to this much effort for my costume for this, did I?" Blake groaned.

"The dance is set to be pretty good," Drew informed.

"Yeah, but that's not due to start for hours," Charlie said.

"We came here for a scare. How about we sneak into the cafeteria, grab some snacks from the buffet, and tell ghost stories in the woods behind the school?" Avery offered.

Excitingly, the group agreed, grabbing what they could before almost getting caught by some of the older students. They ran into the night, to the blackness behind the school.

3

_____

THE GROUP TRAVELED deep into the woods behind the school, arms laden with sodas, chips, candy bags, and sandwiches. Blake had the great idea to swipe a few flashlights to lead the way. And the group laughed at how, when the lights were off, all they could see was the glowing skeleton on Charlie's costume. The skeleton danced a bit as the group laughed, becoming a strange radioactive death, throwing shadows across trunks of trees.

Finally, finding a clearing, they settled into their picnic, occasionally hearing screams from more students visiting Mr. Smith's room. Outside his window, a few nooses hung in the breeze, just out of reach.

They all thought this was a nice touch — unneeded, but clever. The teacher was a pro, most agreed.

One felt a bit less appreciative, however. Alex said, "I expected more from this haunted house with all the speculation last week." Alex was scarfing another cheddar cheese sandwich with light mayo. They had six of these wrapped in cellophane. Charlie was juggling two of them, smiling.

"Well, at least we got a little scare, and now we can have our own fun," Avery said in the creepiest voice possible, sounding like a hoarse creature in the darkness. They aimed their flashlight under their chin and twisted their mouth grotesquely, eyes wide. Their expression seemed both bloated and thin in different places.

"Stop it, you know I scare easily," Drew whined, pushing Avery's lit face away with one hand.

The group laughed. Drew frightened easily but always insisted on being involved wherever the group arranged a Halloween scare or a horror movie marathon. This was a tradition for them.

"I have a story to tell," Alex began.

Alex told the story of a fanged monster that came after naughty children. Apparently, the beast got its list of names from the naughty list of Father Christmas. Just before Halloween, it would stalk the naughtiest prey it could find.

"That's not scary," Blake groaned.

"But wait, you haven't heard the ending. Then, on All Hallow's Eve, the monster would go from house to house and hide under its victim's beds. Clawing, tapping to draw on children's curiosity. Most kids would hide under their blankets, but eventually, they had to put their feet on the floor, and then..."

Alex grabbed Avery's shoulders as the story ended. "It would drag you under with it! .... The last thing you saw would be red eyes in the darkness ... The last thing you heard would be your bones crushing!" Alex was sweating as they yelled.

"You have problems," Avery groaned.

"Monsters under the bed? Really? Man, listen to this," Blake began.

Blake repeated a story Mr. Smith told the year before about the girl in an asylum, accused of witchcraft. She had protested her innocence, but the town wouldn't believe her. "...Finally, after being tortured into giving up her secret on her deathbed, the girl vowed to haunt the people who had hurt her. And when they had given in to her magic, she visited madness again upon the families they had raised. They all had to pay. She spoke of this many times, since the first time they put her in a white straitjacket and threw her in a small, cold padded room to be observed...."

"Why? Why retell that story? You know, it gave me nightmares. You just lost friend points," Drew complained.

The group laughed again before Avery told the story of a girl trapped in a mirror looking for a soul to swap places with her. No matter how hard the group tried, nothing seemed to scare Charlie. Drew attempted to tell the story of a haunted house that no one would live in because it consumed its residents like food, but all the story did was scare the narrator.

"You don't scare easy, do you, Charlie?" Blake asked, grabbing a can of soda.

"Nope. When you have traveled like me, you hear all kinds of scary stories. After that, it takes a lot," Charlie shrugged. Where had they traveled? What did they really know?

"Go on then, if you think you can do better. Scare us," Avery insisted.

"Okay, but you better be prepared because what makes this story so scary is ... it is true." Charlie began settling in and getting comfortable.

"A true story? Do I want to hear this?" Drew asked, suddenly tense.

"You all do. Let's set the scene: It's Christmas nineteen-ninety-nine in Brooklyn, New York. Lauren is a woman living near Prospect Park, a beautiful area. She takes a train and is searching the Manhattan toy stores for that year's must-have toy, a huge plush Mega Force doll. All the other girls wanted Barbies or Tamagotchis — those electronic keychain pets, get me? — But not Lauren; she wanted nothing to do with those Tickle Me Elmo girls." The group vaguely remembered these. Blake's older brother owned a Tamagotchi from back then, barely used it, and said the battery died. Two were fans of the Mega Force games to some extent. They nodded, but tentatively as if they were uninitiated.

"Oh my gosh, do you remember the Mega Force plushie? I wanted one so badly, but it sold out everywhere," Blake laughed.

Charlie paused for effect, catching each of their eyes. "Well, you will be glad you didn't get that toy under your tree that year when I tell you about it."

4

For years, children worldwide had fawned over an animated TV show called The Mega Force Police. The show depicted a group from all corners of the globe, each with special powers, brought together to create the Mega Force Police. Together, they used their powers to battle crimes and save the world and universe from evil foes with similar abilities and alien life forces.

"Like the Power Rangers ...?" Avery whispered. "Shhh!" replied the group.

The Mega Force Police traveled around the globe and embraced cultures and customs specific to their area. As a result, the audience the show reached was immense. The studio hadn't expected their small animation to grow to such an audience, and it wasn't long before the show expanded to a comic book, book series, and toys. Still, the fans craved more.

"Mom! Mom! Look! The Mega Force Police are making a live-action movie! Can I go see it? Can I?" Charlie insisted.

"If you do all your homework, eat all your vegetables and do your chores, I will take you on the weekend," Charlie's mother smiled.

"Thanks, Mom, you are the best," Charlie beamed, hugging Lauren tightly.

The movie was a tremendous success, breaking box office records and launching careers for several actors. With Christmas around the corner, it was only fitting that The Mega Force action figure was being released. Mega Force was a billionaire character who developed their powers after a near-death experience, deciding to take the second chance at life to do good. They sought the rest of their team, picking the eight best superheroes for the job. Mega Force was kind and charming and was everything a kid wanted to be. It made sense that of all the eight characters, while all had a fantastic fan base, Mega Force was the most sought-after toy on everyone's Christmas list.

"Mom! Can I have a Mega Force for Christmas?" Charlie asked over breakfast.

"If you are on Santa's good list, of course," Charlie's father grinned over his newspaper.

"DANIEL, WE HAVE A PROBLEM," Lauren worried.

"What's wrong?" Daniel asked.

"I have searched everywhere online, and Mega Force is sold out."

"You're kidding? Charlie will be crushed."

"I know. When I finish work tomorrow, I'm going to the stores. I just hope I can find one."

The next day, as Lauren finished her shift at the shoe store, she took that train and ran from store to store. She asked so many sales assistants if they had the action figure that all their faces seemed blurred into one. Sold out. She asked about pre-ordering the next batch and reserving one from another store, but each reply was the same.

"Are you kidding, lady? It's this season's must-have toy. I work here, and even I can't reserve one."

Almost defeated, Lauren ran to the last toy store she could find before they closed. A large red arrow encrusted with multicolored bulbs flashed – the Mega Force Police toy line was on the second floor. Unfortunately, the line for the elevator was far too long.

Deciding not to wait, Lauren rushed up three flights of stairs to the Mega Force Police department. Each character had its own section. The entire floor had been dedicated to that line of toys alone. Tsunami, Hitman, Fire King, Wolf, Zara, Professor Dino St. Clair, and Mega Force. Charging forward, Lauren searched through plush dolls, bins of Mega Police buses, water guns in the shape of the Mega Force weapons, costumes, pajamas, and bedroom accessories. There was a line of Mega Force Police apparel, school supplies, learning materials, and much more. One thing was missing: the fabled Mega Force action figure.

That was when she saw it. In a discounted bin, placed there by mistake and poking halfway out, was the only Mega Force left in the store. Lauren ran towards it like her life depended on it. Pushing past shoppers, apologizing for bumping into them, she came up to the bin in a controlled stride...But a young boy grabbed it first and ran over to his mother. Lauren's heart sank, and the world appeared in slow motion as she watched her child's happiness walk to the cash register and out the door.

"Hi, ma'am, how can I help you?" asked the concerned store attendant when she saw the sorrow on Lauren's face.

"Yes, please. I sure hope so. Was that the last Mega Force toy?"

"Honestly, I didn't even realize we had that one left. Sorry, we are sold out."

"When are you likely to get another shipment?"

"Not until after Christmas. Most likely New Year's, in time for the January sale."

"Oh no. I've searched everywhere. Charlie will be so disappointed," Lauren sighed.

"I think there is an old toy store on fifth that might have one. They usually specialize in vintage toys, but it's always worth a try," smiled the assistant.

"Thank you, you are an angel. I'm willing to try anything at this point," Lauren grinned before rushing out and around the block.

Checking her watch, Lauren had fifteen minutes before all stores were due to close. She weaved through traffic, jaywalking and speeding down alleyways, making it just in time. Standing outside the store called The Vintage Toy Emporium, Lauren felt defeated. In the store window were toys from the early twenties and beyond. The store seemed specialized for specific collectors and clientele, a niche store, but Lauren had to try.

A bell rang as Lauren pushed open the door. The store was old and dusty and smelled like mold, must, and centuries passed. Scrunching her nose and clutching her bag to her chest, she was conscious not to touch any of the creepy-looking toys. Eyes followed her as she walked through the store. Everywhere she looked, she couldn't escape the eyes of the past burning into her. She could not recognize even one of the toys in passing their ominous forms on the shelves. She made her way through this chaos to the desk at the back of the store. It was dark back there. Shadows caught upon surfaces as a candle guttered from a corner.

A kind old man sat at the desk with white hair and a green shirt covered in a worn sweater vest. His half-moon glasses sat on the end of a long, arched nose. Lauren thought he might be Japanese.

"Good evening, miss. How may I help you?"

"I don't think you can, I'm afraid," Lauren said, looking around for anything that resembled Mega Man.

"I'll try. What are you looking for?" asked the store owner.

"You don't happen to have a Mega Force toy, do you?"

Surprise spread across his face before his eyes lit up. He smiled. Lauren's worries felt unexpectedly soothed, a weight dropped from her shoulders. She arched up as he began, anticipating.

"You know, it's not normally something I would stock, but one got mixed up with my last delivery. I was going to dispose of it, but here, it's yours. Merry Christmas," the owner said, pulling the must-have toy from under the counter.

"Oh my gosh, I can't tell you how happy you have made me. My Charlie will be so happy. How much?"

"It's yours. Your joy is payment enough," his glasses lowered, peering at her.

"I'M CONFUSED," Alex said.

"Exactly. When you think of creepy dolls, you would think this story would be about one of those vintage porcelain dolls from that very shop. But you would be wrong," Charlie smirked.

"Are you the Charlie from the story?" Drew asked, clinging onto the dragon head of their costume like a comforter.

Charlie paused for a moment before smiling sweetly. "Purely coincidence."

"So, did Charlie get the toy at Christmas?" Blake asked, opening another packet of chips.

"Of course. Lauren got it," Avery pointed out.

"Anyway. So, as I was saying, when you think of haunted dolls, you think porcelain, and most likely, you don't have one just sitting around your home. No one does anymore. But don't get comfortable around any old toy just yet," Charlie continued.

5

"Mega Force Police to the rescue!" Mega Force yelled when Charlie pressed the button on the back of its neck.

"Can I play?" chirped Cameron, who had just turned five three days prior.

"Sure, get your Wolfman action figure. Then, we can play Mega Force Police together," Charlie said, scooping up the toys.

The pair played with Mega Force and Wolfman for hours. Lauren and Daniel were overjoyed that their children loved the toys so much.

For the following months, all they heard around the house were Wolfman and Mega Force's key phrases.

"I will get you and bring you to justice!"

"No one can outrun Mega Force!"

"Bang!"

"Pow!"

"I bet you didn't see that one coming?"

"Mega Force powers activated!"

After a few months, Cameron lost interest in Wolfman, but Charlie was still over the moon with Mega Force. Charlie took the toy everywhere, to school and the park, and once to the zoo. And he slept with Mega Force at his side each night. Finally, Lauren explained that Mega Force was probably best left out of the bathtub, leaving the bathroom the only place Charlie was without it. They had become inseparable.

"I don't think I have ever seen Charlie so enticed by anything before, especially not a toy," Lauren said to her husband one evening over dinner.

"I think you are right. I'm just glad Charlie is having so much fun."

"Yes. Glad I found one."

ALEX, Blake, Drew, and Avery all huddled together, clinging to Charlie's every word. Charlie had a knack for storytelling.

"This isn't so scary. Drew's story was scarier, and we never even got to hear the ending," Alex laughed, poking Drew in the side.

"I'm just easing you in," Charlie grinned.

The crazy glow-in-the-dark costume combined with the flashlights and Charlie's makeup made the grin seem evil. That was the trick to scaring them, as Drew made an audible gulp.

Charlie continued. "He loved that toy so much, that is, until next year when a new must-have action figure came to market. Charlie pushed Mega Force aside, leaving it in the toy box with his other discarded toys."

"Ooooh, the toy is forgotten about and locked in a toy box. So, what does it do to break out and rip the head off the new toy?" Blake mocked.

"Ha! Wouldn't that be fun? But no, just wait. I'm getting to it. You won't be disappointed."

CAMERON AND CHARLIE played in the sitting room in front of the TV. Lauren was busy cooking dinner and humming along with the radio while Daniel read his newspaper in the armchair and sipped his coffee.

Cameron pressed the button on his new toy truck, and the room filled with siren sounds.

"Vehicle reversing! Warning! Vehicle reversing!"

"Ha! That sounds so real," Daniel exclaimed.

Suddenly, Lauren turned off the radio and emerged from the kitchen.

"Can you hear that?" she asked.

"Hear what?"

"It's coming from the playroom. I heard it over the radio. I can't believe you didn't," Lauren said, scratching her head in confusion.

Both parents fell silent and listened closely. Daniel muted the TV to hear a little better. Muffled sounds came from the other room. Confused, Lauren and Daniel followed the sound, and as they drew closer, the sound got louder.

"It's coming from the toy box," Lauren said, opening the lid.

Delving through stuffed toys, building blocks, Legos, and countless action figures, Lauren's fingers neared the source of the noise. It was Mega Force.

"Mega Force powers activated! I will catch you and bring you to justice!" yelled the toy.

"How strange. One of the other toys must have knocked into the button," Daniel said.

"Did I hear Mega Force? Cool!" Charlie cried, grabbing the toy and heading back into the sitting room.

But again, the toy was swiftly forgotten and left with the other toys discarded in the corner. Charlie and Cameron played happily for hours before Lauren declared it was time for bed. While her children slept, Lauren cleaned up the toys, put Mega Force back in the toy box, and organized the others neatly in the playroom. She dusted the shelves and box. Then, satisfied her home was no longer in chaos, she went to bed.

"Lauren! Wake up!" Daniel yawned.

"What's wrong?" Lauren asked groggily as she forced herself awake.

"Can you hear that?"

Lauren listened closely. Her eyes grew wide, and she stared at her husband in surprise.

"Go check!" she insisted, practically pushing Daniel out of bed.

Wrapping his dressing gown around him, Daniel ventured downstairs to the playroom. With each step, the noise grew louder. Daniel feared the worst; he heard the whispering of accents. Was someone in the house? Noises strange to him came from the toy box, muffled. Nervous but also curious, he opened the box. Mega Force sat on top of all the toys reciting catchphrases, but something was different. He picked it up.

"Is it that stupid toy again?" Lauren asked. She had followed him in.

"Lauren! Jeez, you scared the life out of me," Daniel gasped, dropping the toy.

"What did that thing just say?" Lauren asked.

"I don't know. It sounds Spanish... wait, is that Greek?" His parents were Greek, though he was not fluent.

"Probably an unknown feature. I think this toy box is getting too full. Maybe it's time to have a yard sale. Let's go back to bed," Daniel yawned, turning Mega Force into the off position.

"So, the toy kept speaking in different languages?" Drew asked.

"I remember Mega Force, I thought they could only speak in two languages, and you had to pick the action figure with your own language," Blake said.

"Yeah, there was a switch on its lower back, and you could flick between Spanish and English," Avery chimed in.

"Are you guys going to let me tell the story or what?" Charlie complained, fearing they were losing the scare factor.

"Sorry, carry on," Alex said.

Nodding, Charlie continued: "As the years passed, Mega Force would change between languages and randomly start speaking without having its button pressed. Daniel checked to ensure there was nothing wrong with the switch, but the mechanisms were fine. Maybe its electronics were malfunctioning, but the toy kept going as if unhindered. Lauren thought putting Mega Force on a shelf on its own would help. Still, at early hours in the morning, random times during the day, or while they ate dinner, the family would hear Mega Force speak."

"Did they keep putting fresh batteries in it? Most of my toys ran out after a few presses," Drew interrupted.

"That's the thing. The batteries had never been changed. Lauren and Daniel had hoped that the talking would stop when the batteries died, but no — Mega Force carried on," Charlie answered.

"So why didn't they turn it off after every playtime?" Blake asked.

"They did, and sometimes it would be months with Mega Force just sitting on the shelf collecting dust. It's like the doll was crying out to be played with after long periods of loneliness. It was screaming for attention in the only way it could," Charlie answered.

Drew seemed incredulous, but still fearful. "I don't like where this is going ... so go on; what happened next?" Drew asked.

2012

Mega Force was fast becoming a nuisance, creeping Lauren out to the point she wouldn't go into the playroom anymore. Charlie insisted that Mega Force would still be played with every time Daniel insisted on tossing it out. Eventually, Mega Force fell silent. Relieved, Lauren fell back into her routine, no longer suffering sleepless nights or fearing parts of her own home.

One spring day, while cleaning the house from top to bottom, Lauren ventured into the playroom, followed by tunes from the radio in the hallway. Humming along, Lauren cleaned the windows, mopped the floors, and vacuumed the fluffy rug. Then, kneeling next to the toy box, she began tossing toys inside when a sound froze her in place.

"Mega Force activated!"

"Oh lord, not again," Lauren whispered, slowly turning to look at the toy on the shelf behind her.

Lauren trembled, her heart racing as she rose to her feet. She had forgotten she put it there on the shelf, in the open.

"What did you just say?" Lauren asked, instantly regretting her words.

"I'm going to get you ... get you ... g-get you....and bring you to j-j-justice!" Mega Force croaked.

Lauren yelped and ran from the room. Luckily, the door was wide open. Daniel heard and rushed from the garage, searching for his terrified wife, wrapping his arms around her as she cried in his arms.

"Baby, what's wrong?"

Between sobs and gasps for air, Lauren trembled in her husband's arms, retelling what happened as Mega Force repeated its catch-phrase in English, Spanish, German, Greek, and finally Japanese.

"That it, Daniel! I don't care what the kids say. That toy is gone! Get it out of the house, now!" Lauren screamed.

Daniel did as his wife ordered, tossing Mega Force in the trash can in the front yard, burying it deep in the garbage.

Lauren hadn't been the same since that night, so Daniel suggested a trip to his brother's house in Maine to calm her. Happy for the break and distraction of summer, Lauren and Daniel packed up the kids and headed on a well-overdue family vacation.

CHARLIE TOLD the group how the summer in Maine was precisely what the family needed. While catching up on overdue family gossip, soaking up the sun and sea on the beach, and eating good food at picnics, soon all worries of Mega Force had vanished.

Lauren was more relaxed than Daniel had seen her in years. And the couple was able to finally go on an overdue date night or two, thanks to a niece babysitting for them. The bubble of happiness and tranquility abruptly ended a week after getting home. Lauren had a friend stay over one weekend while on a work trip. Lauren's friend hardly slept, insisting someone was talking Spanish loudly outside her window," Charlie said.

"It was Mega Force, wasn't it?" Drew asked, suddenly enthralled by the story.

"Shush, Drew, let Charlie finish," Blake hushed.

Smiling, Charlie continued, ready to deliver the first of many scares.

"Lauren insisted that no one was outside the window. She and Daniel would have heard it, right? Thinking nothing of it, Lauren dismissed her friend's concerns until she went to put the spare pillows and blanket away after the visit."

⚫

"Aaaaahhhh!" Lauren screamed.

Daniel and the children jumped at the alarming sound. Daniel ran to the bottom of the stairs, but Lauren was already sprinting past him into the playroom.

"Which of you two dug this out of the trash?" Lauren demanded.

"What are you talking about? Mega Force is always on the shelf," Charlie insisted, pointing to it.

"I tossed that stupid toy out in the trash before we went on vacation! I promise I'm not mad; just tell me the truth. Who brought it back into the house?" Lauren asked, trying to calm her nerves and sound as peaceful as she could.

"We didn't do it, Mommy. We promise," Cameron said in the most petite voice Lauren had ever heard.

Nodding and leaving her confused children to continue their game of Snakes and Ladders, Lauren headed to the kitchen. She slammed the nuisance toy into the sink. Lauren's knuckles turned white as she gripped the countertop, letting her shoulders sag, panting.

"I believe the kids. They didn't know we had tossed the toy, and why would they go through the trash? Where did you find it, anyway?" Daniel asked, rubbing his wife's tense shoulders.

"On the bench under the bay window in the spare bedroom.

Sonia told me she heard Spanish voices during the night, but I thought nothing of it. So how did it get back in here?"

Daniel thought about it, but he, too, couldn't come to a reasonable conclusion. He shrugged and took the toy back to the playroom. Mega Force was back. Once again, it watched pridefully over the playroom from the shelf, like a kid surveying its kingdom.

7

CHARLIE TOOK a long breath to continue: "At this point, it had been years since Mega Force entered the home. After almost being tossed out and lost to the garbage dump due to multiple disturbances, it appeared Mega Force had learned its lesson. The kids had decided if they wanted to keep Mega Force, they would have to prove that it was still a valued toy. So they started playing with it again. It was like Mega Force had got what it wanted, as suddenly it only spoke when pressed. But something was still wrong. It only ever spoke in Spanish."

"So, if it behaved, why is this a scary story?" Blake complained, losing patience.

"The story isn't over yet," Charlie grinned.

Eyeing the others, Charlie could see that they were still hooked. Charlie knew once the next part of the story was revealed that Blake would be just as enthralled as the others. Blake was just a tough sell.

2014

"Mom, something is wrong with Mega Force. It keeps speaking in Spanish. I don't know Spanish," Charlie complained.

"Yes, you do; you are learning it in school," Daniel insisted, trying to distract from the fact that Mega Force wasn't quite right.

"Yeah, but nothing like its catchphrases. I learned how to say, Where is the library? and My name is Charlie. Not Mega Force powers activated," Charlie groaned.

"Give it here. I will take a look," Daniel sighed.

Daniel took Mega Force to his workstation in the garage. He carefully unscrewed all the parts to take a good look at Mega Force's circuits. Unfortunately, Daniel wasn't the best when it came to modern technology; his children were waiting expectantly over his shoulder, asking, What's that? and Why this? every couple of seconds, which made fixing the toy a bit problematic.

Tightening the final tiny screw, Daniel turned Mega Force back on and pressed the action button. But once again, every word that came out of the toy's speaker was in Spanish. Scratching his head, Daniel looked at the toy and then back at the wide eyes of his children.

"Sorry, kids, I wish I knew what was wrong with it. Maybe just don't press its button. You can make up your own words for it."

"Ok, Dad," chirped the kids, snatching Mega Force and running off to play.

But Mega Force didn't like having its circuitry messed with. And it liked it even less when the kids chose not to press his button so it could speak. As if acting out like a child having a tantrum, Mega Force would interrupt play time by randomly speaking. Its voice sounded harsher and quicker, as if shouting or arguing back.

Charlie and Cameron grew weary of Mega Force and left it at the other side of the playroom, deciding to play cops and robbers instead.

"Freeze police!" Cameron cried out, pointing forefingers at Charlie. "You won't catch me, copper!" Charlie yelled back, retreating behind the toy chest to aim back.

"Mega fuerza policia al rescate! Mega fuerza policia al rescate!

Mega fuerza policia al rescate!" Mega Force chimed in as if wanting to be part of the action.

Startled, the children screamed. They stopped playing, but Mega Force kept repeating itself, each time getting more forceful. Hearing his children scream and knowing it wasn't a playful sound, Daniel ran into the room.

"What's wrong?" he exclaimed.

Daniel's heart sank as he entered the room to see both his children huddled in each other's arms. They were shaking with tear-stained faces staring at the toy across the room, which continued the phrase over and over, screeching. Its voice became the slamming of a hammer against a hoarse bell.

"Daddy, make it stop!" Cameron cried.

"We didn't press its button. It just started screaming at us! Daddy, I'm scared!" Charlie cried.

"I'll fix it," cried Daniel. He picked up the toy and ripped it apart with both hands, its batteries flying from its back. He was angry. To his alarm, the batteries had corroded from years of not being changed. How was the toy still working? How had he not noticed this when he took it apart? It was a question for another day and a concern he didn't want to share with his already scared kids. Batteries removed, Daniel placed Mega Force on the shelf and put a small towel over the top of it, hiding it from sight.

"There, now you don't even have to look at it," Daniel said proudly. He walked off.

"Mega Force wasn't finished yet. Every time someone entered the playroom, it would say poderes activados!" Charlie continued.

"Mega Force powers activated," Avery gasped.

"I've got chills," Drew awed.

"Realizing it was being ignored, Mega Force took matters into its own hands. The family would find it on the kitchen table waiting for them at breakfast, on the doorstep when they got home from school, and sitting on the sofa watching TV after dinner. The TV was turned on," Charlie whispered. The surrounding wind became sharp and fast.

"That's terrifying. What did the family do?" Alex asked.

"Well, naturally, Lauren and the kids were horrified. Lauren was having trouble sleeping, and Cameron began wetting the bed. Daniel couldn't figure out what to do, so he locked Mega Force in a trunk and hid it in the attic...."

Charlie fell silent. A smile like the Cheshire cat combined with his skeleton makeup together was even more terrifying. Alex, Blake, Avery, and Drew sat wide-eyed, waiting. Drew still clung to the dragon head of their costume. Blake was trying to act like the story wasn't that scary. But the fidgeting of empty chip packets gave away Blake's true feelings. Alex sat there, mouth ajar, while Drew had somehow shuffled closer to Charlie.

"Come on, don't keep us waiting!" Drew insisted.

Charlie laughed, scanning their faces and staring back before continuing: "Three mornings went by. I heard no sound from the attic, no voices in the night. All seemed well until Lauren's screams from the sitting room woke everyone in the house. The kids hid under their blankets, terrified to come out. But Daniel went down to check on his wife. When he walked in, he froze dead and was numb."

"Why?" Blake asked.

"Sitting on the mantel was Mega Force!"

8

"SORRY, kids, but this toy is gone!" Lauren said; she was putting her foot down in grabbing the toy off the shelf. She stormed off.

"Good!" Charlie agreed.

"Yeah!" Cameron seconded.

Heading to the kitchen, Daniel grabbed two garbage bags, tossing Mega Force in one and tying it tight before repeating the process again with a second bag.

"Wait! How do we know it won't come back?" Cameron worried, hiding behind Daniel's legs.

"It's garbage day. Come on, let's toss it in the trash and watch it be taken away. That way, we know it's gone for good," Lauren nodded.

Together, the family headed outside. Daniel pulled two trash bags from the trash can and let Lauren put Mega Force in the bottom, quickly piling the rest of that week's trash on top. The family walked back to their doorway and waited.

The garbage truck could be heard from down the street. But as the family anxiously shuffled their feet, it felt like the truck was on the other side of the world. With bated breath, the family huddled together, eyes glued to the trash can, terrified that Mega Force might emerge while they watched.

"Hurry up, hurry up," Lauren whispered.

Daniel hugged his wife a little tighter, pulling his children closer too. Guilt pooled in his stomach. How could he protect his family from something he didn't truly understand and had no explanation for? He felt angry again. After Mega Force had turned up on the fireplace, Daniel had checked the attic. The trunk was still locked and exactly where he had left it. Dust had even gathered on it. He was trying to act brave for his family, but he too couldn't wait to be rid of Mega Force once and for all. He took two deep breaths, holding them briefly.

Finally, the garbage truck pulled up outside their house. The garbage men smiled and waved good morning to the family, who reciprocated with their warmest smiles. The children bounced at their parents' feet as they watched the trash get loaded onto the truck, then roared. Confused, and rightly so, the garbage men looked back at them from their duties.

"They are learning about being greener in school. They wanted to see trash pickup," Daniel joked.

It seemed to be an adequate explanation. With a salute to the kids, the garbage men loaded themselves back in their truck and drove off, taking Mega Force and all the family's problems with them.

"Yay!" the children cheered.

"I think we could all use a break. How about we ... go to Disneyland for a whole WEEK?" Daniel sang.

"What about school?" Lauren gasped.

"I think after everything, we can let them skip a week, right, Lauren? We will just say they are sick. We have been sick, sick about this doll. But kids, this is a one-time thing and our secret, okay?" Daniel said.

"Yes, Daddy!"

"Come on then, let's go have breakfast and get packing. I'll book the tickets while you ready the kids," Daniel said, kissing Lauren softly on the forehead. They felt like they'd taken a new lease on life together.

IT WAS the most popular theme park resort, next to Disney World itself. It had everything a child could want, from wild rides and games to prizes, live shows, and many favorite TV and movie characters were featured. The family made an extra effort to avoid the park section dedicated to The Mega Force Police, which was still at the height of popularity. After all, they didn't need any reminders of Mega Force. That portion of the park felt cursed to them. But they had free rein over the rest.

They spent their days splashing around in the water parks, riding rollercoasters to the point Daniel felt sick, and ate way too much junk food. But, with games for the adults and mini golf, the family had all the fun they could imagine.

Daniel won stuffed toys and new gadgets, and Lauren even treated herself to a few fashion accessories. She had no intention of wearing thunderbolt earrings to work but thought they would be fun when out with the kids.

"This trip was a great idea, and these pictures are going to be an amazing reminder of it," Lauren smiled, looking over the snaps taken on the log flume ride.

"That's the idea," Daniel smiled back.

"I don't think the kids have slept this soundly since they were babies," Lauren cooed. "They were so tired."

"It's all the excitement. I'm a little disappointed our trip is over so soon," Daniel admitted.

"Me too."

WHEN DREW INTERRUPTED Charlie's story to gush about their own memories of Disneyland, Blake and Alex swiftly joined in. Avery listened intently, the group's only member not to have visited the Resort.

"Can I finish my story?" Charlie growled.

"Sorry, continue," Avery nodded.

"So, as I was saying ... The next day, the family drove four hours home. It was still a hot day for mid-fall and arriving home just after lunchtime, they settled in to eat. It was a long drive, so obviously, they were hungry. Suddenly, Cameron heard from their kitchen window a low screeching sound in their backyard. Curious, everyone went outside to investigate...."

"What was it?" Blake asked once again, giving Charlie their undivided attention.

"The family had an old swing set that had started to rust, so the swing made a horrible screeching sound from the hinges. There was no breeze in the air, yet the swing went back and forth...." Charlie continued. "Back and forth."

"How?" Blake asked.

"Sitting on the moving swing was ... was...."

"Not Mega Force?" Drew asked, hiding behind the head of the dragon costume.

Slowly, Charlie nodded.

9

Lauren screamed and shouted a line of profanities. She later apologized to her children for this. Then, ushering the children inside, Lauren left Daniel to deal with this "thing." She was bewildered and beyond frustrated. The children ran inside faster than she could follow. She instead walked into the front door, looked back, and slammed it behind her. She almost locked it but caught herself.

When Daniel opened the door and walked in empty-handed, not knowing what more to do, Lauren ushered the kids into the sitting room and closed them inside so she could cry. She sat at the table sobbing, her head in her hands, pulling at her hair. Lauren felt she may have a nervous breakdown; she didn't know how much more she could take. Her husband felt the same way.

"Daniel, what are we going to do? Every time we toss that thing out, it finds its way back. How is it back here, and how on God's green earth is it swinging on a swing? Do you think one of the neighbor kids is pulling a prank on us? I bet it's the Bentley's kid Rory. They've always been a mischief maker. I'm going to go and have words with their parents right now!" Lauren rambled, jumping from her chair.

Daniel rushed across the room, taking his wife by the shoulders, pulling her close and trying to calm her.

"It's not Rory. How could it be? We watched the trash collectors take it," Daniel offered. He was breathing in deeply again. The anger and confusion was replaced by something indiscernible. He was in deep thought and barely listening.

"Then what explanation do you have, Daniel? I'm at my wit's end; I can't take this anymore. We are just going to have to sell the house. It obviously likes it here, so let that stupid doll keep the house, but I'm not staying here a minute more. I'm taking the kids and going to my mother's."

"You can't do that; what about school?" Daniel asked.

"Oh, so it was okay for you to take the kids out of school to go on a mini vacation? But not okay now for me to take them out of harm's way?" Lauren snapped.

"Lauren, calm down. We are not in danger. It's just a creepy toy. It hasn't done anything to us but scare us. We can figure something out."

"Like what, Daniel? Everything we have tried has failed. I'm going to go mad over this. I can't take it anymore! Isn't it enough to be scared? To fear for your damn sanity?" Lauren sobbed. Daniel felt like a bad husband in these moments, powerless in his role. He was a strong and smart man with a beautiful family, but he felt the fool.

THE FRIENDS SAT BACK, debating how Mega Force could have come back. They tossed around ideas to try and explain the toy's odd behavior. But just like the family Charlie described, none of them could. The only thing all could agree on was that Mega Force was haunted or cursed with some form of life.

Charlie continued to tell the story. Lauren and her family hardly slept. She became irritable and snapped at her children and husband for no reason when arguments occurred. Every family member grew scared of their own shadows, eventually sleeping with every light in the house switched on. No one had brought Mega Force back inside. But at night, the swing could still be heard swinging, with Mega Force reciting its famous words into the still air of mornings and on cold rainy nights, again and again, and again.

"Eventually, one of the neighbors knocked to complain about the "toy that was talking" into the night. They claimed having noticed it on their swing weeks prior and said they were as patient as the next person, but it had to go. Lauren and Daniel were careful in explaining their issue, but the neighbor laughed in their faces and told them to "just deal with it," or they would be "calling the police with a noise complaint," Charlie said.

"So, what did they do?" Drew asked.

"Well, Daniel's job was important," Charlie answered. "He couldn't have a police incident on his record, so he pulled the doll back into the house. Lauren stuck to her word; unable to live in a house with the toy, she took Cameron and Charlie to stay with her mother until Daniel could figure out what to do with it."

Charlie went on to explain how Lauren and the kids would video call Daniel, hoping for updates every night. But Daniel was no closer to figuring out what to do with the toy. He was getting frantic about it, about the noise and his family leaving. He thought of quitting his job but could find no reason to do so besides that he was stressed by the noise. He had taken the doll apart and cut all its wires clean, locked it in several bags and back in the trunk in the attic, and even buried it in the yard. But somehow, when Daniel got up, Mega Force was waiting for him every morning, its innards fully intact. Daniel swiftly started to understand what Lauren was talking about – the madness of the situation and the conversation floated between them about selling the house. But selling the home would be a lengthy process, and Lauren and the kids didn't want to be away from Daniel for that long. That's what Lauren told him, at least. He did not feel reasonable about most things anymore — even his family.

"But things went from bad to worse," Charlie said. "One night, when Lauren and the kids were on another video call with Daniel, about to wish him goodnight, Cameron started crying. It was a sudden low whine from a grown man, not something they would do. Lauren asked what was wrong, and Cameron pointed to a section of the screen just behind Daniel's head. Mega Force had miraculously turned up on the fireplace mantel as if joining the conversation." Charlie gasped for dramatic effect.

"DANIEL! Please, I beg you: something needs to be done about that doll. I'm scared not just for the kids and me; I'm worried for you and your safety too," Lauren pleaded.

"I'm trying, Lauren, believe me. I promise I will have a solution soon," Daniel said.

But even as he made the promise and the words left his lips, he knew it was a lie. What could he do? What hadn't he tried? One evening, when Mega Force's catchphrase echoed in Spanish around the house, Daniel woke up in tears. Bounding downstairs, he hunted high and low for Mega Force, finally finding it on the shelf in the playroom.

Sitting at the kitchen table, staring eye to eye with the toy, Daniel felt foolish in trying the only thing he could think of, something that seemed like a last resort.

"What do you want? Why won't you leave us alone? I miss my wife and kids. I just want them to come home! Please let them come home!" Daniel begged and pleaded between sobs.

Daniel waited, staring at the toy in the center of the table; it was motionless and dead silent for the first time in years. Anger again spread through Daniel like wildfire, heating him to the core. It was toying with him.

Grabbing Mega Force around the waist, Daniel snarled at the toy, baring his teeth. Spit flew from his mouth. He put his jaw upon the toy's head and bit down with the power of an animal tearing meat from a carcass. He pulled it away from his face at a meter distance.

"I hate you! You ruined my family!" Daniel roared, almost losing his voice, tossing Mega Force across the room.

The toy hit the wall, creating a dint in the plaster, falling to the floor with a loud plastic crash against the hardwood. Daniel panted, staring, waiting for something — some reaction, some retaliation, a verbal response, anything ... He couldn't understand his motivations about this anymore. Mega Force lay still and face-up on the floor.

10

2020

After another sleepless night, Daniel rested his waist against the bathroom sink. Looking back at him was a man he barely recognized. His hair was unkempt and greasy, his beard overgrown in unruly tufts, and he could have sworn those gray hairs around his temple were new. Looking back was a man whose face had aged by stress and time. He saw eyes deep into their sockets, dark with circles, like cave entrances.

Going for coffee, Daniel was surprised to find Mega Force face down on the kitchen floor, exactly where he had left it the night before, with plaster from the wall scattered around. Unable to take his eyes off the toy, Daniel sat at the kitchen table, holding his coffee continuously. His stomach growled from hunger, but he couldn't bring himself to cook, let alone eat. He needed to find a solution, or he would waste away and never see his family again. They would not have him like this. That's when his phone rang. Digging the cell out of his pocket, he saw a name that made him sigh a breath of relief. It was his older brother Simon; Simon always had a calming effect on Daniel.

"Hi bro! How are you, the wife, kids? I hear you have had a bit of a tough time lately. I spoke with Karen and Michael; what's this I hear about trouble with a toy?" Simon laughed.

Sighing, Daniel didn't know where to start.

"Bro? You all right?" came Simon's concerned voice.

"Not really, Simon," Daniel answered.

Over a long conversation, Daniel explained all about Mega Force, from the day that Lauren found it in the creepy vintage toy store to the first time they noticed something was wrong. Daniel told his brother everything, how Lauren had taken the kids, the neighbors had complained, and how the toy seemed to have a mind of its own and always found its way back. Daniel even confessed to talking to the toy the night before. He left out having bitten into it. The anger of that moment was embarrassing, but at least Daniel knew he could still feel embarrassment.

"You serious?" Simon asked.

"I wish I wasn't," Daniel said.

Suddenly, Mega Force started spouting phrases in rapid succession, all in Spanish.

"Damn!" Simon said. "... To be honest, I thought you were losing your mind or something when your wife told me about it. But, tell you what, mail the toy to me. I'll take the problem off your hands."

"I couldn't ask you to do that, Simon."

"What are older brothers for? Besides, my kids love this kind of crazy stuff."

Finally, with a solution on hand, Daniel called Lauren with the good news. Mega Force would be out of their hands shortly. But as expected, Lauren said she wouldn't return until she was sure Mega Force wouldn't show up one morning on the fireplace.

"So, Daniel wrapped Mega Force in bubble wrap, bagged it, taped it into a box, and shipped it off to Utah," Charlie began to wrap up the story.

"Wait! Here? Your story ends here, in Utah?" Drew looked panicked.

"I told you it would be scary," Charlie laughed.

"So what? Did Mega Force come back? Did Lauren and the kids come home?" Alex asked.

Nodding, Charlie explained how once Simon had received the package, he had immediately tied Mega Force to the bumper of his truck. Then, every day, he would take a picture with the toy still attached to the truck and send it to Daniel as a sort of status report.

After several weeks of Mega Force not moving, Lauren and the kids finally returned home.

"Well, I'll give you this, Charlie. It had its moments, but it's not the scariest of stories," Blake shrugged.

"Yeah, the ending was a little anti-climactic. I expected you to say Mega Force broke free and headed back or killed the new family or something," Avery said.

Charlie smiled and shrugged, saying nothing else. Suddenly, Charlie's phone rang, breaking the silence and causing the rest of the group to yelp. Laughing, Charlie answered the phone and swiftly ended the conversation.

"That was my dad; he will be here to pick me up soon," Charlie said.

The group nodded, a little disappointed that the night was ending. Charlie had homework to do and wasn't the biggest fan of school dances, so they had never planned to stay the entire evening.

"Wait! Charlie, so was the story about you?" Drew asked.

"No, but fun fact: Charlie is a very popular name in my family," Charlie winked.

Slow, heavy rock music hummed in the distance, and truck lights shone through the trees, indicating the night was truly over.

"Well, nice try, Charlie, but you need to work on your ghost story skills," Blake mocked.

"Noted," Charlie laughed.

"Ready, kid?" asked Charlie's dad, popping his head from the truck window.

"Ready, Dad. See you later, guys," Charlie said, jumping up and dusting the debris from the floor of the skeleton costume.

"Wait! Charlie, isn't your Dad's name Simon?" Drew asked.

With a wicked smile and a nod, Charlie ran to the car. As Charlie jumped into the passenger side, the group gasped. Heavily strapped to the bumper of Simon's truck was Mega Force.

"It's not the same doll from the story. Charlie made the whole thing up to try and scare us; of course, they tied some doll to the truck," Blake mocked.

"Mega Force powers activate. Mega Force poderes activados!" Mega Force blurted out. Simon's truck pulled away; the noise from the thing was constant and died off slowly, like a raid siren, swelling and echoing.

All at once, the group jumped to their feet as a cold shiver ran down their spines. They sprinted back through the woods toward the school, passing under Mr. Smith's window nooses. Charlie sat in the passenger seat of their father's car, smiling, knowing that the group had indeed got the scare they intended.

"*Llevarte a la justicia*. I'm going to get you and bring you to justice!" Mega Force's voice echoed through the woods after them.

The End

Did you enjoy *Ghost Stories*?
Please consider leaving a review on on this platform or on
Goodreads, Bookbub, or your favorite bookstore.
Reviews help me reach new readers.

Join my Newsletter to get a FREE book.
www.mhlebeault.com

ABOUT THE AUTHOR

Positive, uplifting books and stories.

Marie-Hélène Lebeault is the author of *The Evers Series, Clarity Castle, What Happens Next? Readers Decide Which Story Becomes a Book, the Blood Magick Trilogy, Holiday Shifters, Ghost Stories, Defenders of the Realm, Utopia, Chronicles of the Starborne Cadets, Legends Reborn,* as well as a series of picture books called Fairy Grandmother. She lives in Canada with her grown children.

www.mhlebeault.com

Follow on Social Media, she'd love to hear from you!

facebook.com/mhlebeaultauthor

x.com/mhlebeault

instagram.com/mhlebeault

amazon.com/author/mhlebeault

bookbub.com/authors/marie-helene-lebeault

goodreads.com/mhlebeault

linkedin.com/in/mhlebeault

tiktok.com/@mhlebeaultauthor

ALSO BY THE AUTHOR

North Pole University - Paranormal Romance

Holiday Shifters

Freshman Frost

Sophomore Solstice

Junior Jinx

Senior Spark

Legends Reborn (Fairytale Retellings)

A Curse of Snow and Ash

A Curse of Thorns and Slumber

A Curse of Glass and Shadows

A Curse of Scars and Silver

The Chronicles of the Starborne Cadets

Confluence of Destinies (Prequel)

Stars Beyond Realms

Shadows of Orion

Echoes of the Void

The Nebula's Heart

The Starborne Paradox

Defenders of the Realm

A Journey to Power

The Quest for the Emerald Rattleback

A Summer of Discovery

The Quest for the Sacred Tree

A Summer of Opposites

The Quest for the Phantom Feather

A Summer of Courage

The Quest for the Kraken's Ink

A Summer of Destiny

The Quest for the Cursed Mirrors

A Summer of Unity

Defenders of the Realm - Special Edition Hardcover Set

The Evers Series

The Ancestors' Key

The Academy

The Time Walker

The World Jumper

5th Anniversary Edition Omnibus

The Traveler's Handbook

The Lost Key

Blood Magick Trilogy

The Blood Mage

Blood Magick

Blood Legacy

Extended Edition Omnibus

Standalones

Clarity Castle

What Happens Next?

Ghost Stories

Holiday Shifters

Echoes of Tomorrow

Utopia

Picture Books

Fairy Grandmother: Millie Goes to Antarctica

Fairy Grandmother: Millie Goes to the North Pole

Fairy Grandmother: Millie Goes to China

Fairy Grandmother: Millie Goes to Africa

(Also available in French, Spanish, German, and Italian)

www.ingramcontent.com/pod-product-compliance
Lightning Source LLC
Chambersburg PA
CBHW032014240626
47153CB00003B/1246